Operation Condor

by
Albert Norman

Order this book online at www.trafford.com
or email orders@trafford.com

Most Trafford titles are also available at major online book retailers.

In this work of fiction, the characters, places and events are either the product of the author's
imagination or they are used entirely fictitiously

Note for Librarians: A cataloguing record for this book is available from Library
and Archives Canada at www.collectionscanada.ca/amicus/index-e.html

Printed in Victoria, BC, Canada.

ISBN: 9781-4251-013-0-5

*Our mission is to efficiently provide the world's finest, most comprehensive
book publishing service, enabling every author to experience success.
To find out how to publish your book, your way, and have it available
worldwide, visit us online at www.trafford.com*

Trafford rev. 08/17/09

 www.trafford.com

North America & international
toll-free: 1 888 232 4444 (USA & Canada)
phone: 250 383 6864 ♦ fax: 812 355 4082

This book is dedicated to Caroline Beehn of Yuma Arizona and Mary Gregory of Gibsons, BC.

"A million thanks to my granddaughter Erin Norman for the final editing"

Chapter 1

IT WAS IN Berlin 1935. Herman Goering, who was a director of Deutsche Lufthansa, the German National Airline, invited Adolph Hitler to a social event held for the pilots and heads of the Airline. Just recently, Hitler, through a military takeover, had elevated himself from the position of Chancellor to the position of Dictator.

Goering, who had distinguished himself as a decorated ace during World War I, was still interested in aviation. The Treaty of Versailles forbade Germany from forming a military air force. Goering, with Hitler's blessing, started up the Berlin Flying Club. To start with, the club trained their pilots on gliders gradually advancing up to small light aircraft and eventually achieving their pilots' licenses.

Most of the original instructors were pilots from the original German Air Force and had fought in World War I. Even though the club was supposed to be a private organization, the instructors were paid from a subsidy received from the federal government, as were the funds for purchasing the aircraft and equipment.

Several of the instructors and senior members were Lufthansa pilots who had gained considerable experience flying the big bombers during World War I. One of these was Captain Albert Wirth, now flying the large Junker Tri-motor JU 52 aircraft to the major cities in Europe such as Moscow, Paris, Madrid, Rome and London as well as the major cities in Germany. In Africa he flew to the northern cities such as Cairo, Tunis and Tripoli and down the west coast to Casablanca, El Aaiun and Dakar.

Right after World War I he was hired by Lufthansa to fly the Junker F13. It was the first all metal, predominantly corrugate aluminum, constructed aircraft with a single engine and full cantilever wing. It was an airplane that was far ahead of its time. Most of the airlines from other countries were still using modified World War I type aircraft that were mainly constructed from wood and fabric. Much of the military type transports didn't offer significant comfort to the passenger, whereas the Junker F13 had a nice enclosed cabin and good visibility for the four passengers. The early transports didn't fly great distances; they were only in the air for a couple of hours so there was no room or need for flight attendants.

In 1930 Captain Albert Wirth was appointed second officer and co-pilot on the famous Dornier DOX multi-engine flying boat that was flying between Hamburg and New York City, USA. The DOX was more of a ship with wings; it was the largest plane in existence when completed in the summer of 1929. It had twelve engines mounted on top of the wing, six pushers and six engines as tractors. During the first flight trials at Lake Constance on October 21, 1929 there were 169 persons on board, a crew of ten, 150 passengers and 9 stowaways. During these early days of flying there was a problem using land planes; the airports were small with few facilities so the trend was toward the use of flying boats for more passenger comfort and larger payload. The experience of flying across the Atlantic played a very important part later on in Captain Albert Wirth's life.

The big tri-motor Junker (JU52) that Captain Wirth was flying in 1935 usually carried twelve passengers and a co-pilot/steward. He flew to cities all over Europe and Africa. Consequently, the company had to set up refueling and maintenance stations throughout Europe and Africa.

It was at the 1935 social that Hitler met Captain Albert Wirth. Before the social Hitler had Goering make up a dossier on all the people he was going to meet. The one person who intrigued him the most was Captain Albert Wirth because of his international experience and war record.

"So, Captain, how long have you been flying for Lufthansa?" Hitler asked, even though he had studied the Captain's dossier for the past two days and he knew everything he wanted to know about this handsome pilot. Captain Wirth was over six feet tall, had blonde, curly hair with blue eyes that expressed his strong determination and ability to be in control.

"I started sixteen years ago, Mein Fuhrer," Albert answered cordially.

"Do you like making the long flights - and please relax, I'd like this to be a pleasant social?"

"Yes, I've always enjoyed the flights to interesting places throughout the world, especially the ones on the Dornier DOX." After answering, he thought to himself, why did I say that? Actually, he enjoyed the flights to Africa the most because there was so much to see. It was just something in Hitler's manner that made him blurt it out.

"That is very interesting, because I'd like to discuss this topic with you at greater length. Have you a card so I can contact you?"

Upon receiving the card he studied it momentarily, gave Captain Wirth a smile and said, "You'll be hearing from me."

Albert had been associated with senior officials for many years and had never been intimidated by any of them. This discussion with Hitler gave him a very strange feeling about his fate and future after meeting this powerful man.

It was just after his next trip to Africa when he was having his layover rest that he received a personal phone call from Hitler himself. He was asked to come to Hitler's office at noon and have lunch with him.

This request coming so soon after the social puzzled Albert. He was trying to figure out what Hitler was up to and hoping he was not a homosexual. "No, not that, not Mein Fuhrer." He considered this but was ultimately unconvinced of this notion, although the invitation was puzzling.

The next day he took a taxi to the Federal Government Building where he was led into Hitler's office promptly at twelve o'clock. Hitler greeted him warmly with a double clasped handshake and led him over to a table that had two chairs and indicated for him to take a seat. While doing so he carried on a friendly conversation.

"How was your flight? Where did you go?"

"This one was to Senegal, Africa. It's the nearest place on this side of the ocean to fly to South America."

Now why did I add that? Am I being led into something? Albert worriedly thought.

Actually Hitler knew exactly where and when Albert had been to Africa. How could this man know what was in Hitler's mind because Hitler himself hadn't formed a final plan yet? Was it just coincidental or maybe the captain had a plan of his own? Time will tell. Hitler decided to keep pumping this man for further information and not divulge what he had in the back of his own mind.

"Have you ever flown across the Atlantic to South America?"

"No, I haven't, but I think the airline should start considering plans to extend their route to South America. I know from talking to other pilots that France has an air -mail service that goes all the way to Buenos Aires, they haven't started a passenger service yet but I understand as soon as they get the right aircraft they will establish a passenger service, which could be in a year or two. Portugal has been flying their naval planes to Brazil and several of the islands in the South Atlantic for the last year or so. They also are planning to extend a passenger service to South America."

"Do you think it would pay for Lufthansa to extend to South America?" Hitler asked inquisitively.

At this point a waiter wheeled in a dinner cart bearing what smelled like a delicious luncheon. Albert held off his reply until the waiter finished serving both positions.

Once the waiter had left, he answered,"Very few new routes pay off at first, but it may be wise to do a survey run to determine the feasibility. Of course it all depends on the type of aircraft we have, to make good payloads and operate efficiently. I'm sure we will have such craft in a few years hence. We are making great strides in the industry."

"The largest passenger carrying airline is England's Imperial Airways--their service covers most of Europe, North and South Africa, all the way down to Cape Town. They also travel through the Middle East and over to Karachi, India. They are just embarking on an extensive program to use large flying boat type craft, which provide luxury accommodation. However, seeing that England is an island, it is understandable they would tend toward using flying boat type craft, but I feel that improved land transport planes will eventually carry most of the passengers and be able to land anywhere in the world. I understand there are such planes on the drawing boards of the manufacturers at this moment--it is just a matter of improving on the motors, aircraft components and equipment. The airplane industry is going ahead in leaps and bounds."

Hitler pondered this for a moment, considering the feedback he had received: "I appreciate your well thought out remarks, Captain. Now let us enjoy our luncheon. We shall have more discussions on this subject at another time."

Albert wasn't too surprised when he received another phone call from Hitler's office. It was the message that caused him some concern. He was instructed to be at the Head Office of Lufthansa the next day at one PM. Now he wondered: "Did I say something wrong to the Fuhrer? Am I in trouble?"

The next day he took a taxi, a little earlier than necessary, to the Lufthansa Office at the Tempelhof Airport. He wanted to sit outside the office in the Airport waiting lounge to observe any strange happenings or to find out what he was in for. Several of the Lufthansa brass had passed by; some, upon noticing him, gave him a friendly wave or nod. So far so good, it didn't look like he was there to get fired. At one PM he went into the company office and was immediately led into the Board Room. The secretary pointed to a name card to indicate where he was to be seated. The designated position had a nice, big, leather covered seat. It was next to the chairman's position at the end of the table. As Albert glanced around he noticed that Herr Goering was not present. Hitler later explained to Albert that Goering has been transferred to the Federal Government's head office as Director of Aviation Production. Germany has just made a pact with Generalissimo Franco of Spain to supply the Spanish rebel side with military aircraft. This was one way of getting around the Treaty of Versailles; they couldn't have an air force but there wasn't anything in the Treaty about constructing aircraft for another country. Germany was taking advantage of this loophole, not only to tool up their factories for military aircraft, but also to use Spain as a testing ground and a place to train fighter pilots.

Just as he got seated, the door to the President's Office opened. Everyone in the room rose at once and to their surprise, not the President, but the Fuhrer entered.

Behind Hitler came a secretary carrying a stack of binders, which she distributed to all the positions. Then she left the Boardroom closing the door behind her.

Hitler then addressed the meeting.

"Gentlemen, I have just appointed the president of Lufthansa, Herr Ludwig Wagner, to the position of Deputy Minister of Public Works. As many of you may know, Ludwig is a brilliant civil engineer. Germany is in a vast program of civil development and his service is required in his new position."

"If you all will look in your binders you will see the agenda for this meeting. The first item is the financial report. Please read it and make any comments pertaining to it."

Two of the directors suggested the budget be cut back even though the airline was showing a marginal profit. Some of the others indicated they agreed.

"Then I take it, gentlemen, you wish to cut off or reduce your salaries." As Hitler said this he was looking at Albert, who couldn't hide the slight smile on his face.

Immediately there was some quick blustering and back pedaling by the Directors, indicating they wished to withdraw the suggestion.

"Gentlemen, most of you probably know Captain Albert Wirth. I invited him to join us. I have had some very interesting discussions with the Captain. By the way, Captain, what do you think about the Financial Report?"

"Quite frankly, I am amazed to see we have made a profit when I think of all the bungling that has gone on." He thought, oh, here I go again, opening my big mouth.

With his cold blue eyes and with his Captain's authoritative attitude he looked straight at the directors. He noticed there were several nervous look-aways. He had hit a big nerve.

"Thank you, Captain, for that honest and direct reply." The Fuhrer seemed oddly pleased with Albert's assertiveness.

"By the way gentlemen, I have appointed Captain Wirth President and Chairman of the Board of Lufthansa. I can see the company needs new and experienced input. Please give him your full support. I am sure the next report will be very interesting."

Hitler stood up and as he left the room he gave a nod and a look to Albert as if to say "It's all in your hands now -- go to it."

Albert didn't hang around; he didn't want to be compromised by anyone. He headed for a tavern away from the airport. He wanted to be alone to think things over. He never figured it would come to this, even though he knew some day he could end up in management.

Later that afternoon after he had a chance to think things over, he went back to the airline Head Office where he was introduced to his secretary and office staff. After settling down in his office, his first order of business was to have the secretary send a notice to the Chief of Pilots. This was the first official notice of Captain Wirth's appointment as Chairman of the Board of Lufthansa. It was to advise of Albert's new position and that there would be no immediate changes in the operation. He also asked for the Chief of Pilots to select a replacement pilot.

As soon as he could, he phoned to his girlfriend, Frieda Schmidt, a nurse at the hospital in Dusseldorf. It struck him as he was phoning that Hitler never asked him if he had a girlfriend. Why not? Actually, Hitler knew all about Frieda. She would eventually be part of his plan. Albert didn't mention his promotion while talking to her on the phone. He wanted to save that information as a surprise for her. Frieda was about five foot six in height with a nice slim figure, dark hair and violet eyes, giving her a very striking appearance.

Albert had been invited to attend a friend's birthday party in Dusseldorf, a month before he met Hitler at the Lufthansa dinner. When he was introduced to this beautiful woman their eyes locked and a magnetic attraction took place. They spent the rest of the social talking and inquiring about each other. They had both lost their parents due to sickness during the war. Frieda was fascinated with Albert's flying experiences. She happened to mention that she had never travelled outside of Germany and would like some day to take an airplane trip.

Albert had dated Frieda a few times; he would use his airline pass to fly to Dusseldorf whenever they both could get time off to see each other. He would take her to nice restaurants and the movies; they enjoyed each other's company. She would make sure it was a romantic movie they selected. They would sit at the back of the theatre where he could put his arm around her and she could put her head on his shoulder, without having abusive remarks directed at them from patrons behind them. It was the place where they could enjoy a kiss in the privacy of the theatre. Albert's love for Frieda grew more each time they met. He was glad to get the promotion to head of the Airline because he was starting to get love-sick. Quite often lately he would find himself dreaming of making love to Frieda and forget he was flying an airplane, which could be very dangerous. In his new position he would be able see her more often, making for a happier and safer situation.

Realizing that Germany was now involved in the Spanish Civil War, the airline's office and servicing arrangements would have to be moved away from Madrid. It was now a war zone and therefore not safe for airlines to fly there, especially German ones.

Albert decided to move the Lufthansa passenger and service depot from Madrid to Toulouse, France. The city of Toulouse was the centre of French aviation construction and the headquarters of the Airline that provides airmail service to South America. The small airplanes they were using have to carry a large petrol load in order to make the long flight across the South Atlantic from Dakar to Natal, therefore they only had space for the mail and light parcels.

He decided to take an inspection tour of their facilities and make new arrangements for servicing their planes and the passenger facilities. He planned to use a single engine Junker transport that had been equipped with long-range fuel tanks. He would fly it himself to Toulouse and then further on into Africa to set up Lufthansa service depots.

While planning the trip to Toulouse he sent a letter to the head of the hospital where Frieda was a nurse. He requested two weeks leave for Nurse Frieda Schmidt. He explained in the letter that the Airline was planning to use nurses as stewardesses on the airline and needed the input from Nurse Schmidt on this matter.

Albert phoned Frieda before he sent the letter to the hospital asking, "How would you like to go on an airplane trip into Africa?"

She said, "I sure would, but I don't think I can get enough time off."

"If you could get the time off, would you take the trip with me?"

"Albert, you know damn well I would, but how can I get the leave?"

"You just leave that part to me. I'm going to send a letter to the hospital administrator requesting they give you leave for a study on using nurses as stewardesses on Lufthansa. Of course it'll be on Lufthansa letterhead stationery."

"You could get fired for doing that."

"No I won't, because I AM the President, CEO of Lufthansa."

"You're kidding! When did this happen?"

"Oh, did I forget to tell you? Last week."

"You didn't forget, you knew that when you phoned me last week. I could tell by the tone of your voice when you called that you had something on your mind, you bloody smart ass! That was what you were planning, to get me to run away with you?"

"Then I take it, the answer is no?"

"Don't tease me. Of course I'll fly away with you."

Actually the heads of the hospital knew that Nurse Schmidt and the airline pilot were dating. Now, when they realized he was not only a pilot but also the President of Lufthansa, there was no hesitation in granting her leave. They didn't want to get involved politically.

He phoned and told her how long they would be away for and where they were going. Also he would fly the plane to Dusseldorf and pick her up at the airport. This was just the break they both had been waiting for since they met at that party.

It was a clear warm day when he landed at the Dusseldorf airport. He had given the Dusseldorf office instructions as to when they were to pick her up at her apartment and take her to their office in the airport. They treated her like royalty, knowing she was somebody important. Albert wasn't quite sure how Frieda would take this invitation to go away with him to France and Africa.

"A business holiday trip or a rendezvous?" Frieda wondered.

He waited in the plane as one of the airline officials escorted her over. One glance at her and he could tell it was going to be a perfect trip. She was smiling and looked more beautiful than he ever imagined. He greeted her at the door of the plane and while the porter was putting her luggage in the plane's outside hatch she threw her arms around Albert and gave him a great big loving kiss. They held onto each other like two lovers would, trying to make up for the time they had been apart and finding it hard to believe this was really happening. He took her up forward and got her seated and buckled up in the co-pilot's seat, then he carried out the cockpit check list procedure. When satisfied everything was OK, he started the engine and taxied out to the end of the runway and waited for the Tower to give him the clearance for take-off. He had Frieda put her head phones on after he got her settled into her seat, so she could hear the Tower talking to him. When she heard the Tower give permission for them to take off, she turned and gave Albert a big grin and smile; she was really enjoying the whole thing with no sign of being nervous. He knew now this was going to be a perfect trip.

They took off at 9:30 AM for an about two and a half hour trip to Toulouse, just in time for lunch and to check into the hotel. He leveled off at two thousand meters knowing that the commercial planes flew around three thousand meters and smaller craft one thousand meters altitude. Even though it was a beautiful clear day and Frieda was enjoying the flight and the view he was being careful and was following visual flight rule.

After about an hour into the flight Frieda started to study the cockpit and the controls. She appeared very interested, asking a lot of questions. Albert decided to give her some instruction. First, he explained the instruments, then the controls and how they worked. Finally he got her to take a light hold on the control wheel and both feet on the rudder pedals as he did the controlling, so she could get the feel of the plane. He also told her to watch the instruments as they did banks, turns, ascents and descents. He was amazed as to how quickly she caught on to handling the plane and to understanding the instruments and the controlling.

He corrected the plane's direction, then turned the controls over to her. She flew the plane for the next hour and he took over for the approach and landing. In a way, he was sorry that she was so excited about flying the plane; he thought maybe she might fall in love with the plane instead of him.

Just before they landed he asked her if they should have separate rooms.

She asked, "Are we going to get married?"

"Yes, of course."

"Then you register us as man and wife."

He thought: "I never in all of my years figured that a marriage proposal would be so simple. Who proposed to whom?"

After he checked them into the hotel as man and wife, he phoned the Toulouse City Hall and set up an appointment for the next afternoon. Then they went and had an enjoyable lunch grinning at each other with happiness.

That night she not only proved she was a virgin but she left no doubt in his mind as to whom she loved. Now he realized for certain that it was he she loved and not the flying of the plane.

Before going to bed Albert used the washroom first, then while Frieda was getting ready for bed and using the bathroom Albert lay in bed waiting in anticipation for his first love to join him. She came out wearing a very sexy negligee and before getting into bed laid a big towel on the bed while giving Albert a sexy smile and explaining she didn't want to mess up the bed. For the first time since they met he could feel the warmth and softness of her body. This is what he had been dreaming of since he met her and it was more thrilling than he had imagined. Before making love she said not to worry about taking precautions because she had to douche anyway. She'll take care of the clean up. At this point he was glad she was a trained nurse, so that they both could enjoy themselves to the utmost.

It took all the next afternoon to make the arrangements with Toulouse City officials for a Lufthansa Passenger Terminal and Service Station there. Frieda spent the afternoon doing some tourist type shopping and observing the city and its people. They had a late supper, which was customary in the southern country, then stayed in the dining lounge to listen to the hotel orchestra and dance to the romantic music.

"How did you make out with the city officials?"

"Much better than I expected. I got a very good deal on the lease agreement; they realize how important it is to have a major airline using their city as a terminus and service depot. How did you make out shopping?"

"Well, the shopping was interesting, seeing as how I don't speak French, but those Frenchmen, I think they thought I was a new prostitute in town. I couldn't tell what they were saying but I had no doubt what they wanted. It was very interesting."

The next morning they took off to go to the Lufthansa station in Casablanca. Because of the war in Spain they had to fly east to the Mediterranean Sea, then skirt around Spain down past the Balearic Islands.

As they flew along the southern coast Albert explained about all the historic and scenic points of interest making it very enjoyable for Frieda's first trip to this part of the world. Pretty soon she lost interest in the scenery and bugged him to let her handle the controls.

He turned the controls over to her while flying over the sea towards Casablanca. She now had about one hour flying time at the controls and was learning more about the plane's other controls and instruments--such as the valves for switching to reserve petrol tanks, reading the compass and adjusting the trim controls on the rear plane or stabilizer. Albert thought that a few more days of this and Frieda will be able to land and take off. She's the best student he had ever instructed, better and faster than any of the ones at the Berlin Flying Club. Maybe it's because she is sleeping and making love with her instructor, giving her more than the usual confidence.

They were approaching the Casablanca airport just after twelve noon. Albert asked Frieda to again hang lightly onto the controls as they prepared to land. He gave instructions as to adjusting the throttles to make the plane descend, to switch on the carburetor heat control that would prevent the carburetor from frosting up and causing the engine to stall, which could cause a crash. Above all she was to watch the airspeed instrument when coming in for a landing. If the airspeed got lower than 95 km the plane could stall from the lack of airspeed and crash. Frieda showed no signs of fright when told these instructions. She followed right through with him on the approach and landing. He taxied the plane right up to the Lufthansa service tarmac. When they got out he gave instructions to the service foreman to have the plane fuelled up, checked over and readied for flight the next morning at 8 AM.

Casablanca is a very romantic setting, with a warm tropical breeze gently moving the palm trees and the air sweet with flower fragrance. After lunch they were sitting on the hotel lounge patio under an umbrella having an afternoon cocktail of red wine while they discussed the trip.

"Have you given any thought as to when the wedding should be, Albert?"

"Yes I have, there are some things we have to discuss."

"Oh, so you got me into your bed and now you want to back out?"

"Nothing of the sort. I love you too much to think that. Do you like flying the plane?"

"Yes, what's that got to do with our marriage?"

"Everything. If we hold off on our marriage I can send you to flight training at the Berlin Flying Club. When you get your license I'll see to it that you get on the Airline as a co-pilot stewardess. Then you can fly the big transport planes after you have been properly trained. What do you say?"

"Boy, you sure drive a hard bargain! I can see why you were made head of the Airline. OK, but don't try to back out on me or I'll run a prop up your ass."

They both were laughing and enjoying themselves in this romantic setting, knowing they have plans for an exciting future.

The next morning when they got to the airport Albert showed Frieda how to do a pre-flight inspection of the plane and sign in the logbook when everything checks out. This was a job she would have to do, even on the big transports, whether she's pilot or co-pilot.

They were now headed for Dakar in Senegal on the west coast of Africa where several of the other airlines were using Dakar as their terminus. Some time ago Albert thought it might be better if the Airline had its own terminus a little further up the coast in a little town where they could train the help to be exclusive for Lufthansa. That was the reason for this trip, to speak to the Sheik in charge and set up a depot--one they could eventually use for crossing the Atlantic.

The first night they stayed in the main hotel in Dakar. It was very hot and humid so they stayed most of the evening in the bar and dining room where the overhead fans gave some relief from the tropical discomfort.

The next morning they went by taxi out to the airport to give instructions to the ground crew chief. Albert wanted the plane thoroughly inspected, maintained and readied for the long flight back. When Albert finished checking out their office and facilities he instructed the taxi driver to drive them up the coast to the next village. Even though the taxi driver understood and spoke French he questioned Albert about the instructions explaining that the road to the next village was quite primitive and rough. Albert asked him if it was passable. The driver gestured with his hands meaning, maybe yes, maybe no. Albert told him to give it a try and he would pay for any damage to the vehicle. The driver gave the "French shrug" and started the journey. Fortunately, it had not been raining hard, so even though it was rough with muddy patches, the trip took about an hour and half. They went right to the Sheik's palace and after giving his President and CEO Lufthansa card to a servant he explained he wished an audience with the Sheik. France as French West Africa controlled this part of Africa so there was no problem with communication because Albert was fluent in French.

Albert asked Frieda to remain in the outer waiting room while he had the meeting with the Sheik. He explained that women were not accepted in meetings in most of Africa and he asked her if she wanted to wait out in the cab. She said she preferred to be inside where it was cooler.

Albert was impressed with the Sheik's private office which was quite modern with expensive furnishings. The Sheik met him at the office door and greeted him with a friendly handshake, then asked Albert to have a seat at a nice chair in front of the desk. He then asked him if he would like a cup of coffee. Albert said, "Yes thank you," knowing that the coffee would be rich and sweet. He didn't want to offend the Sheik by refusing the gesture. Before leaving Berlin he had the secretary make up a contract and a letter of proposal laying out a request to allow Lufthansa to establish a service and passenger depot in this little seaport town, called Rinsque. He presented the letter to the Sheik while they were having their coffee.

Looking around the office he noticed that the Sheik had an extensive library of good books in several languages and he was obviously well educated by his choice of words and vocabulary. For some reason Albert took a liking to the Sheik. There was something relaxing and gentle about him.

After the Sheik read the letter, he asked Albert where he was staying.

"The wife and I are staying at a hotel in Dakar."

"Herr Wirth, I'd be honored to have you and your wife stay here as my guests. I think it would be wise, because there are many things we should discuss. You don't have to worry about transportation; I'll have my chauffeur take both of you back when you are ready."

Fortunately Frieda had insisted they take small suitcases when they left the hotel in Dakar. She said, "You never know what might happen or where we could get stuck overnight when travelling in this foreign country." It was good thinking on her part.

Albert explained to a relieved and pleased Frieda that they were invited by the Sheik to be his guests while negotiating the terms for setting up a terminus.

Albert paid off the taxi driver and thanked him for bringing them to Rinsque. One of the Sheik's servants took their bags from the taxi into the small palace where he led them to their quarters and mentioned that the Sheik had invited them to have lemonade with him out on the palace garden terrace at five o'clock before going to dinner.

"Please advise His Highness that we are delighted and shall join him at five o'clock."

The suite was quite large and nicely decorated with a deep pile Indian rug over the ceramic tile floor and the walls had expensive paintings. There was a ceiling fan quietly circulating a breeze throughout the room. The architecture was Moorish in design and had double balcony doors opening out onto a private patio.

The bathroom was of modern design with a one and a half meter by two and a half meter fully tiled shower that was big enough to hold two to four people. They enjoyed a refreshing and much appreciated shower together.

While they were getting dressed Albert enlightened Frieda on some of the customs and religious beliefs of the people in this part of Africa, such as no drinking of alcohol. They respect women of a different religion, but prefer they don't interfere with male discussions unless asked to participate.

Albert warned Frieda, "Probably we'll be using European cutlery but if he is eating food with his hand, watch which hand he uses and do the same."

A servant led them out on to the patio where the Sheik was waiting for them. He gestured where to sit on either side of him. Before they sat Albert said: "Your highness, I'd like to present my fiancée, Frieda Schmidt." Frieda was surprised that Albert introduced her as his fiancée instead of wife, but she realized he was being honest and laying all his cards on the table.

"I'm very pleased to meet you Frieda Schmidt. If I'm not being too impertinent, is the wedding soon?"

"Well, not soon enough for me, but Albert says I have to learn to fly first." They all had a good laugh, breaking the ice and creating a friendly atmosphere.

After spending a pleasant hour drinking lemonade and carrying on a friendly conversation, finally there was the tinkling of a dinner bell, the sheik rose and said, "Come, let's have dinner."

Both Albert and Frieda were pleased to see an elaborate layout of European style place settings. The servants brought in large bowls of food which they served into each person's plate, asking if they wished for more. It was European fare: chicken with dumplings and gravy, along with a variety of vegetables. The dessert was sliced peaches served in crystal dishes. The beverage was a delightful fruit punch or Arabian style coffee.

The sheik carried on a friendly conversation during the meal, making his guests feel comfortable and relaxed.

"By the way my friends call me 'Em,' short for Emile, which is my European name. I'd be pleased if you wish to call me that."

Albert took a liking to Em. It became evident the Sheik was well educated which prompted Albert to ask: "How many languages do you speak, Em?"

"I speak six languages. I attended Oxford, Yale and the Universities in Berlin and Paris. My father was a wise man and he insisted I obtain a good education. My disciplines were language, mathematics, history and business administration."

Albert now realized he will not be dealing with an ordinary person, but one who has much more intelligence than anticipated;

he hoped it would help to make a good transaction for the Airline.

Em was reading Albert's thoughts. He knew Albert was here to negotiate a business agreement and he didn't want to appear to be too anxious but he is quite willing to hear what the airline has to offer.

"I'll have the beverages brought out onto the terrace where we can relax and discuss why you are here."

When they all got settled down on the terrace chairs around the patio table, their refreshments were served.

"OK, Albert, why are you here?"

"I'm here to discuss the setting up of a private maintenance depot for Lufthansa. We are planning to set up a depot here on this side of the Atlantic to service our overseas flights."

"I see, but why here instead of Dakar, where the other airlines are setting up their depots?"

"I'd like to set up our own service facilities instead of having to depend on one that is a conglomerate of other airlines. We have tried the amalgamation system before and it wasn't always satisfactory. Especially now with the political unrest in Europe it might not be wise."

"Did you bring a contract that we can discuss?"

"Yes, here it is," Albert said, taking it out of his suit coat pocket.

Em laughed, "You sure came prepared. Are you the signing officer and is this all your idea?"

"Yes, Em, I'm it, the one responsible and the signing officer."

"OK, you two relax while I go over this contract. I guess my father was correct when he insisted I take Business Administration at the university," he said with a wink and a chuckle.

"It appears to be a good offer but I'd like to sleep on it tonight. Is that OK?"

"Yes Em, I think it would be wise. We want everything properly understood and to have a good relationship with you.

Would you want payments sent here or do you prefer somewhere else?"

"I have an account in Switzerland and I shall note it in the contract as the preference along with the account number."

Chapter 2

WHEN ALBERT AND Frieda went to bed that night, she looked over at him and said. "What are you smiling about? I can tell by the conversation you two had that things are going quite well."

"I'll explain it all on the flight back home, but needless to say, I am very pleased."

The next morning at breakfast Em presented the signed contract along with his Swiss bank account number.

Em asked Albert: "When do you plan to start construction of the terminal?"

"Well, Em, it depends on when I can get the contractors lined up to build the complete set-up, that is, the hostel for accommodation, the office and hangar. Do you know anyone that would be interested in taking on the job?"

"Yes, as a matter of fact, I have a fellow in mind who's a Danish fellow named Andersen, and he is the representative for some oil companies. He has had to have contractors throughout Africa do construction work for his business. I still have your business card, I'll have him contact you and I'm sure he can take care of the construction for you."

They shook hands and toasted the occasion with their morning fruit juice.

Right after they cleaned up and packed their bags the servant took the bags to the Sheik's big black Mercedes. They all gave each other friendly handshakes as Em said, "Now remember, when you come down to open the facilities, both of you are to be my guests, and as for you Frieda, I'd like to hear that you flew the plane to here." He gave that sly wink of his as he waved good-bye to them.

The trip in the limousine back to Dakar was a lot more comfortable than the taxi trip down.

They arrived at the Dakar airport about ten AM. The plane was all fuelled up and ready to go. After Albert did the pre-takeoff ground inspection, he warmed the engine up and did an entry into the log. He then did a last minute check of the instruments and gauges making sure there was a full tank of petrol then tested the controls. When he was satisfied everything was ready they taxied out to the runway, did a visual check to make sure there was no aircraft approaching, then gunned it for the takeoff.

It was a clear bright day, because they were taking off too late to make it to Casablanca during daylight. Albert decided to land at El Aaiun as he wanted to inspect this little town half way up the coast to Casablanca. They should arrive there just after lunchtime; plenty of time to inspect the facilities and do some sightseeing and maybe some shopping.

They leveled off at thirty-five hundred meters. He could feel Frieda staring at him; he turned and grinned at her.

"Do you want to take over now or would you want to discuss what happened with Em?"

"Don't be funny, the news about Em can wait until tonight when we are in bed. Let me fly this thing." They both were laughing and enjoying the trip.

Approaching El Aaiun, Frieda relinquished the controls to Albert when she realized she has still a lot to learn, especially how to side slip a transport plane into a low approach landing on a small field such as the one at El Aaiun. After seeing the plane was secured in the hangar they headed to the hotel which was a comfortable walking distance along a narrow street with Arab merchants displaying their wares in the Bazaars. This was all new to Frieda; she enjoyed the shopping, even though Albert had to do the bargaining for her in French. She was pleased with a well-made leather purse he bought her-- it would have cost much more in Berlin.

That night in bed she said: "OK, why the happy face and smiles about the meeting with Em?"

"Did you notice how he requested the payments be made to him?"

"Yes, to a Swiss Bank account."

"You know everything has gone better than I ever expected, meeting the Sheik, Em, getting the lease, possibly a contractor to handle things at Rinsque and a contact with a fellow in the oil distribution business. It's all falling into place. I wasn't surprised, but I've had a premonition of what's in store for us. I think we will have a wonderful future, trust me."

She replied, "I have to trust you. I'm stuck out in the middle of the desert with you." She grinned at him and tried to figure out what he was thinking about.

The next morning after maneuvering on the ground to get in position for a difficult takeoff from the small strip, he had to give ten degrees more flap, rev up the engine to full throttle before releasing the brakes, then get the maximum lift to miss some trees at the end of the short runway. Once safely in the air they turned north and headed for Casablanca.

The flight up the west coast of Africa wasn't without rough air bumping them up and down. The wind off the ocean became turbulent when colliding with the hot desert air. Albert made sure their seat belts were on and done up tight. Frieda was glad she was doing the flying because it kept her mind busy concentrating on the handling of the plane and too busy to become airsick. It was a good experience and practice for her on how to handle an airplane in rough weather. She was thankful that she was not a passenger on this rough flight. She also realized what to expect when she becomes a pilot. It's a good training exercise for her.

When they reached Casablanca they did a circuit around the airfield, checking the windsock for wind direction and to observe if there are any planes on the field or in the air. Albert let her handle the landing along with his instructions and him hanging lightly onto the dual controls. He was very pleased with her performance; he realized she had the ability to learn and adapt to the handling of complicated equipment without getting flustered, and she will make a very good pilot.

They had a late dinner out on the hotel terrace. It was comfortable with a light breeze fanning them from the ocean. They remained out on the terrace after dinner drinking gin and tonic and discussing their trip in Africa.

"When do you think we can do this trip again?" Frieda asked.

"I think it will probably be next year some time, after you get your commercial pilot's ticket. I'll have to make another trip to Rinsque to finalize the installation of the Lufthansa depot there. By the way, what do you think of this trip, have you enjoyed yourself aside from flying the plane?"

"You know Albert, if someone told me a year ago that I would be taking an airplane trip to Africa and sleeping with a handsome pilot, I'd probably have hit them with a bed pan.

You asked me if I have enjoyed myself--well here we are, sitting on a terrace overlooking the Mediterranean Sea in this romantic setting of palm trees with a warm tropical breeze coming off the ocean and that big bright moon shining its silvery path across the water to us. I've been treated like royalty since the start of this trip, and in a few minutes I am going to go to bed with my handsome prince so I can make love to him and show him how happy and appreciative I am."

"I'm glad you have enjoyed the trip. It certainly has been a wonderful trip for me. I have enjoyed every minute of it because I had you as my co-pilot and lover. I know you'd like to get married soon, please trust me, whether you get your pilot's license or not we will be getting married as soon as possible. This is our last night of the trip; tomorrow we will be getting an early start and will be in Dusseldorf by dinnertime. I know you are pleased with yourself for flying the plane and I am very proud of you--you'll make a great pilot--but not a word to anyone. It could cost me my job and my license and even our marriage. Now let's celebrate our last night in Africa and enjoy ourselves."

They took off from Casablanca early in the morning. Frieda did the taxiing out to the takeoff strip while Albert did the final checklist before takeoff. As a safety measure Albert held lightly onto the dual controls. Frieda eased the plane into flight at the correct airspeed, climbed smoothly to one hundred meters then did a banking turn and headed east down the Mediterranean. Albert was looking at her, he was not only in love with this lovely creature, but was very pleased with the way she has taken to flying an airplane. He was still wondering, "Does Frieda love flying an airplane more than she loves me?" She was the best student he had ever instructed, a natural pilot, and he was proud of her.

He plotted a course going east in the Mediterranean south of the Balearic Islands. He wanted to avoid getting too close to Spain because of the Civil War that was raging there.

They were off Barcelona flying across the Gulf of Lions south of France, heading for Marseille, when suddenly two Fiat fighter planes appeared, one on each side of them. Albert noticed they had the insignia of the Spanish Rebel Air Force. He told Frieda to act friendly towards the pilots. They were both waving to the pilots of the fighters. Frieda said, "They are both taking turns flying past my side. They are throwing kisses to me and I'm throwing kisses back to them."

"Good girl, just keep flying steady on this course. We are making good time, must have a tail wind, and we should arrive in Marseille around eleven o'clock. If we are lucky and they are not too busy we should be able to get serviced and head for Dusseldorf before lunchtime."

Albert told Frieda that he'd have to take the plane in because this airport is one of the busiest in Europe. They came in from the sea over the city, did a full circuit over the airport, noting the planes on the field, ones taking off and landing, and when it was clear they landed.

When they got to the service tarmac, Albert asked Frieda to get the thermos filled with coffee and pick up some sandwiches from the airport restaurant. He wanted to head for Dusseldorf as soon as the plane got serviced. If they got a tail wind, they should arrive there around five o'clock and have time for supper before taking Frieda to her apartment.

When he leveled off at two thousand meters he turned the controls over to Frieda who was biding her time until she could take control. At this altitude they were running into patches of heavy clouds, making visibility intermittent and the air a little bumpy. Albert asked Frieda to climb up higher to look for clear air. They came out on top of the clouds at three thousand meters. This was the last chance Albert had to give Frieda unofficial instruction. He regretted that the trip will be over soon as it had been very enjoyable with Frieda acting as a student pilot, and the romantic time they had together. The satisfactory business arrangements made with the Sheik has justified the long flight into West Africa. He had a strong feeling Hitler will be satisfied with his report.

As they started to descend to Dusseldorf Albert said,"I'll have to take it from here to the landing. The controllers in the tower have binoculars and will be watching our approach and landing. I've already spoke to the tower over the radio, they've given us clearance to land but have warned me to watch for other air traffic and to switch on our landing lights, so other planes can see us in the air during our approach."

Albert taxied up to the Lufthansa hangar. After giving the Lufthansa service manager instructions to have the plane serviced and ready to carry on to Berlin, they had dinner at the Airport restaurant. They were feeling kind of sad that the holiday trip was at an end and they were going to have to separate for a while.

"OK, what's the plan now?"

"The first thing I'm going to do right after making my report to Hitler is getting an apartment for you. I hope to get one near the Berlin Flying Club, so that it will be convenient for you. I've never seen the one you have now. What is it like?"

"Well it isn't really like an apartment, more like a shoebox. It's a little one room that I share with another nurse. The bathroom and phone are out in the hall; anything larger that you can get, would be better and I'd sure appreciate it."

"I won't make any promises, but I'll do my best to get you something decent. It may take a few days so be patient, I'm sure it'll be better than what you have."

Albert ordered a taxi for Frieda, gave her money to cover the fare and tip, then after a big hug and kiss he promised to get a place for her in Berlin. He'll phone as soon as everything is ready to move her. Also he mentioned that she should advise the hospital that she'll be resigning.

When Albert went into his office the morning after he arrived back in Berlin, he noticed his secretary gave him a funny smile as if to say, "I know what you have been up to." It started the wheels of thought working in Albert's head, wondering if there was a spy system being carried out in the office that was reporting about him to someone. He had an idea who it could be and it wasn't Hitler. That day he made his report to Hitler, explaining his meeting with the Sheik and presented the signed contract. Hitler was very interested about the Swiss Bank account and how it worked. He asked Albert why he chose Rinsque and was it a suitable location for flights to South America? Albert explained his reasons for choosing Rinsque. He wasn't surprised when Hitler agreed with him and thanked him for a good report, confirming his original feeling about a plan being hatched by someone else.

Albert stayed late after work after having a suspicion that something was going on with a certain Director and the secretary. After everyone had left the office he decided to do some checking up. He thought the office records could reveal some misdemeanor. When he tried to check the office file he found it was locked. He searched the secretary's desk and finally found the key hidden under a drawer. He pulled the financial reports going back for the last six months and the expense submissions of the directors.

He found several items that didn't balance out with the financial statements. It was quite obvious that a certain Director was doing some skimming and with the help of the secretary who was juggling the reports. Maybe they were sharing the loot, or was she blackmailing him for something?

Albert had scheduled a nine AM Directors' meeting for the second day after he arrived back from the trip. That morning he was at the office by 7:45 ahead of the rest of the staff. When the secretary arrived he instructed her to be present at the Directors' meeting to do the minutes.

Albert was ready for the attack. The Director that had bullied his way in previous meetings, without addressing the Chair, made an accusing speech. He said, "This new President has taken it upon himself to waste the Company's funds by taking his girl friend on an African holiday. I move he be told to resign his office in disgrace." He sat down with a smug smirk on his face sneering at Albert.

There was dead silence. The others were stunned. Albert, for what seemed like five minutes and was probably only a few brief seconds, just gave the Director a cold stare without blinking.

Then he said; "First of all, you have one hell of a gall making a statement without addressing the Chair. Second, you have loaded the Company with your useless relatives and cronies. Third, I am calling for a full audit of all spending. You're going to be lucky if you don't go to jail. Fourth, I'm kicking you off the Board as of immediately. You are to leave the premises as of right now and do not take anything with you. This meeting is adjourned. The rest of you will be notified when the next meeting is scheduled." As he walked out he could hear some laughing coming from the Board Room and someone quipped "Good riddance."

Right after the Directors' meeting Albert made his report to Hitler. When Albert described what happened at the meeting, Hitler laughed as though he had been told a real good joke. He slapped his hand down on the desk while laughing. He said he wished he had been there to see the face of that Director when he was kicked out of the meeting. He said he never did like that arrogant person; it was Herman who appointed him to the Board. He told Albert that the person had powerful connections and that he will try to make trouble for Albert. He advised Albert to press charges as soon as the audit is complete to protect himself.

That afternoon Albert purchased the latest edition of the *Berlin News*, to look up the ads on apartments for rent. He picked one out that was close to the Berlin Flying Club and went to inspect it right after having lunch. He was quite pleased with it upon inspection: it was a fully furnished suite, self-contained, with its own bathroom and a separate bedroom. He knew Frieda will be pleased with this choice because she told him hers is only a one room tiny apartment with no facilities. He also realized it was bigger and better than his own apartment and will eventually be theirs when they get married.

There was no problem renting the suite. Evidently the big shiny auto Albert was driving, especially when he gave his business card to the manager, impressed the manager very much.

He phoned Frieda that night to give her the good news about the apartment. She was full of questions about the apartment but Albert would only say that it was adequate and that he thinks she would approve of it. He wanted her to be pleasantly surprised when she sees it. Another plus was the fact it was within short walking distance to the Flying Club so no transportation problems for Frieda.

The next day he drove to Dusseldorf to pick up Frieda and move her to the apartment. He helped her carry the few possessions she had, mostly clothes. He realized she should be very happy with her new abode, after seeing the little room she had been living in. She kept pumping him all the way back to Berlin about the apartment. He just kept saying, "It's nice, I think you might like it."

When they were first unloading the auto, getting ready to move her things into the apartment she still hadn't seen inside yet. He unlocked the door, turned and carried her into the suite. She dropped everything she was carrying and threw her arms around his neck, and with tears of happiness, she kissed him and whispered, "Thank you," while clinging to him.

There was no food on hand so they went out for dinner and later on bought groceries to fill the empty shelves in the apartment.

It was getting late when they got back to the apartment so Frieda convinced him to stay the first night with her. They broke in the nest, like two lovers should do.

That night in bed he mentioned that when he was in the Air Force his companions called him Al and he would like to be called that. She agreed and stated that it suited him. She liked Al.

The next morning he noticed there was no secretary on hand when he went into his office, but there was a letter on his desk. It was from the one who was his secretary. She had resigned due to ill health. He thought, "Good, now I don't have to fire her. I'd better notify the Steno Pool that I need a secretary." He hoped to get a good one.

A few days later he took Frieda to the Berlin Flying Club and signed her in as a new member and he, as her sponsor, introduced her to the Chief Instructor, and then he departed back to work. She was shown around the facility then given a summary of the training.

The first two weeks she was to attend Ground School classes, learning the basics of aviation, meteorology, navigation and air regulations. She had to take textbooks home and study for an examination. Al coached and instructed her so that she passed her exam with high marks. She enjoyed it very much, realizing this was more fun and interesting than studying to be a nurse. After passing the first exam there would be the primary flight training, flight instructor's test and exam, the training for a student pilot license, finally a pilot's certificate, then building up flying time, studies and training for her commercial ticket.

Al had warned her repeatedly not to mention about knowing anything about airplanes, or ever touching the controls of a plane before. They knew it's going to be difficult keeping her experience a secret but she'll have to say she has read a lot about flying planes and let them think she is a naturally good student. He warned her again it could cost him his job if it ever leaked out that she flew the plane with him. This whole thing could be made political and become very messy. There was naturally going to be gossip and suspicion about her ability to learn so fast. She couldn't socialize with any of the other students or Club members.

Frieda expected to start flying lessons in one of the training planes parked outside of the Club House. She was kind of disappointed when an instructor took her out to a two place soaring glider used for primary flight instruction.

After showing her the controls, how they worked, and the instruments, a tow plane towed them aloft - it was quite a sensation. After releasing from the tow plane they drifted quietly and soared like an eagle. Any thought about disappointment evaporated when the instructor turned the controls over to her. She had to pretend that she was a little awkward at first, but her ability to fly soon took over. Luckily the glider was not powered so it didn't appear too obvious; she had to learn to fly using the Glider Method.

The instructor was very impressed with her progress. When they landed he asked her, "Have you ever taking flying lessons before?"

"No, why do you ask?"

"Well, you're the quickest learner I have ever had."

"I have been intrigued with flying ever since I was a child and have read all sorts of books about it."

The instructor was curious and he asked about the books she had read, but she skillfully sidestepped the topic.

It only took a week of dual instruction flying the glider before she was allowed to fly it solo.

Next was the dual instruction in one of the training planes, and again it was a thrilling experience flying in an open cockpit biplane, wearing goggles and helmet. She felt like a World War I fighter pilot. It only took two weeks of dual training before they allowed this eager fledgling to go at it solo. She had to write another exam and take a flight test with an inspector to get her first pilot's license with no problems.

In order to get her commercial ticket it took about two months of flying instruction and tests, and she accomplished all this with great victory.

Chapter 3

ON SEPTEMBER 15, 1935, Frieda Schmidt got her Commercial Pilot Certification Ticket. That night, she and Al celebrated by drinking champagne, dining and dancing. While they danced she asked, "Now can we get married?"

"Do you want to fly the big transports?"

"Yes."

"The marriage has to wait until I can get you on as a pilot at Lufthansa. There is an opening coming up on one of the Junker G38s. There are two of them, they are the flag ship of our fleet, they have a crew of seven and carry thirty-seven passengers. They fly to all the major cities in Europe. When the present captain retires the pilots will move up one rank. I hope to get you on as Third Flight Officer, but I'm thinking of hiring you right away to fly co-pilot on a Junker 52 Transport so you can build up some time on transports."

Frieda was glad to hear she might be flying transports soon, but a little disappointed that marriage will have to wait.

Al had a long time friend, Peter Wasmuth, who used to be a pilot in the Air Force and eventually became a very successful merchant in Berlin. One day while they were having lunch at Peter's Club, Al asked Peter to accept the position of Director on the Lufthansa Board as there was that vacancy from the firing still to be filled and the board could use Peter's expert knowledge of business.

At the next board meeting Al introduced Peter to the other members though they all knew of him and accepted him as a good acquisition to the Board. The air transport business was expanding quickly all over the world. Lufthansa had been dragging its feet for the last four years and now it was time to get moving and catch up to the other countries that had been advancing in aviation. Lufthansa needed new and aggressive thinking on its Board so it can play a part in Civil Aviation. Peter had been involved in aviation since World War l. At his first board meeting he came up with some very good suggestions.

One suggestion was that Lufthansa sponsor a ladies' airplane race from Berlin to Marseille, France, and back. He mentioned the British sponsored the Mac Robertson Race, London to Melbourne, Australia last year, and that the USA had their big International races each year. He suggested Germany have an International Women's Air Race in the springtime before the Berlin Summer Olympics. Al asked Peter if he would make a motion to his suggestion, which Peter did, the others all agreed and it passed.

Peter also suggested Lufthansa do some updating of their Fleet, such as purchasing some of the new Heinkel Transports. He mentioned this to the Minister of Finance to purchase and that he expected to obtain at least six by the end of the year.

Al asked Peter if he would be Chairman of the Ladies' Race, strike up a committee and get everything set for next May (1936). Peter agreed and he even offered to donate a cash prize for the winner. Peter was a charter member of the Berlin Flying Club, he was also the President and Chairman of the Directors. At the next meeting he saw to it that a motion was made and passed that the Club Sponsor a Ladies' International Air Race from Berlin to Marseille, France, and back to Berlin. The race was to be in May of 1936 and be open to all countries.

It was decided to make it a one-event race for speed. A lot of European countries and North America have been racing prototypes of fighter planes for the last few years, so the Directors thought by having just one high-speed event it would attract the countries with their fastest planes and best women pilots. Peter offered to put up cash prizes for the first three places and the Lufthansa Directors agreed to donate a big trophy for the winner. After one of the meetings, Peter was talking to Al about the race; he asked Al if Frieda will be entering the Club competition to see who will represent the Berlin Flying Club. When Al affirmed that Frieda would enter and probably be flying one of the Club's Junker type 86 sport planes, Peter said: "The JU86 is OK for the Club race, Al, but I'll see to it whoever represents the Club will be flying the Messerschmitt 108. It's a prototype of Willy's new fighter, the 109. I'll sponsor it for the Club, but of course it'll have my company's name painted all over it. The USA will most likely have Jacqueline Cochran with her big Seversky and Madeline Dubois from France will probably be there with that very fast Caudron. Both of these women have won races and they will be the ones to beat. Frieda will have one thing to her advantage and that's you. You've flown over the territory for several years and probably can give Frieda several good tips and advice. The Berlin Flying Club is going to promote the Race; it'll go over the wire services and be in the papers all over the world. Six women members of the Club have signed up to enter the Club Competition Race, so the Directors decided to have a cross country race to decide who flies the 108. It was decided to have a Race to Magdeburg which is about 100 km from Berlin around a well known landmark, Church Steeple, and back to the Berlin Flying Club. The winner will be the one to fly the 108."

On a clear day in April 1936, at nine AM with all the six Club contestants on hand, they drew out of a hat for their order of flight. Frieda drew number six, which Al was hoping she would get because she would know which time she had to beat to win. On the previous practice flights Al had kept track of the times it took Frieda to do the course.

Number 4 and number 5 were good pilots; these are the ones Al was concerned about. Number 2 came in way under the time Al had recorded. He concluded that something was not right so he got the head judge to phone the Magdeburg tower judge to check if number 2 had made the flight around the tower. The judge stated that she hadn't but he saw with his binoculars and heard a plane fly around the tower on the north side of town and that so far there had only been one flight around the official tower.

When the announcement was made the woman's husband became very belligerent and tried to claim they were cheating his wife. The head judge put him on the phone to the tower official to confirm that there had only been one plane recorded so far but the guy still thought his wife should be declared the winner even though the rest hadn't flown yet. Four and 5 came in under the time Al had recorded. Number 5 was now the fastest time and that's the one Frieda had to beat.

Now it was Frieda's turn. She must have shoved the throttle to full wide open as the JU86 roared down the flight strip. She kept it so low Al thought she was going to plough it through the farmer's fence. He also heard the chief mechanic moan and mutter something about a complete engine overhaul.

When Frieda got to the tower she did a diving turn. The judge said she went around it so close and fast he barely had time to identify it. She did as Al suggested by climbing slowly up to 4,000 meters, held that altitude until she had the Club airstrip in sight then she dove wide open down to the field. She flashed past the finish line and did a victory barrel roll, a loop, and descended for a smooth landing. She beat number 5 by three minutes. There was no doubt in the Club members' minds that Frieda was the one to fly the 108. Al was very proud of her and he knew she was proving to everyone that she was good enough to be a transport pilot.

The next day while Al and Peter were having lunch, Peter said, "I'm concerned that the 108 will not be fast enough for Frieda to win the race."

Al asked with a trace of concern, "What do you suggest?"

"I've been considering talking to Herman about the Club getting one of Willy's 109 Fighter prototypes as an advance trainer. We will be needing one soon for our Reserve Force. If we can obtain one soon enough, then Frieda will have a better chance of winning than if she was using the slower 108. I'll talk to Herman this afternoon and let you know what happens."

That evening Peter phoned Al after his meeting with Herr Wilhelm Messerschmitt and Herman Goering. Willy had just finished doing the test flights on the 109 and he had agreed to install a more powerful engine in it. He wanted it to be the fastest plane in the race and hoped it would break the world's speed record for land planes.

Peter said, "Both Willy and Herman were very enthusiastic about having the 'souped up' 109 entered in the race. They both have been trying to find a way to promote the 109, so they can get several for the Club as advance trainers. Everything is fitting in place; the Club will have the 109 in a few weeks and in time for Frieda to do her check-out flights and a test run to Marseille and back. Willy has offered the use of a 108 for Frieda to do her advance dual training in. I think it would be wise if you'll be her instructor for the race."

When Al told Frieda the news, she was very excited about it and asked a lot of questions about the 108 and the 109. The next day Al obtained the specs for both planes and started to give her the basic instruction for both planes. Also, he got the navigation maps for the flight route and started to coach her on the readings and flight path. They were going to be very busy for the next two or three weeks.

The 108 is a side by side dual control plane that is almost identical to the 109 except for its power. It has a retractable landing gear and wing flaps like the 109, so it is a good plane to be training in for the faster 109.

Al brought Hitler up to date on the plans for the race. Hitler expressed his pleasure about the race and especially the part about using the 109 to win. He agreed to present the Lufthansa Trophy especially if Frieda Schmidt won it. He said it would be a great day for Germany if Frau Schmidt won the Race. It would finally make Germany one of the leaders in aviation and would help to promote Lufthansa, especially if Frieda became a pilot for Lufthansa.

Al thought, "There he goes again, reading my thoughts and plans."

Within two days, a 108 was delivered to the Berlin Flying Club. On that same day Al started to check Frieda out in it. She had to study all the instruments and different levers, such as the lever for the flaps and the one for raising and lowering the landing gear. There was no time to lose; they even started the checkout flight that same day. Al was very thorough and business-like with his instructions. This was the most important part of his plan to get Frieda employed at Lufthansa as a pilot, and then they could get married.

Within the week they made two trips to Marseille and back. She had to do the navigating and all the flying, especially the landings and takeoffs using a check off list. She hadn't enough hours or practice to do it by memory, so she had to do it the Lufthansa Transport way, with a check list and no room for errors.

Finally Frieda had to solo in the 109, but she wasn't concerned because she had piled up hours in the 108. The 109 had a lot more power, which was quite noticeable on takeoff. Al had to instruct Frieda to ease the throttle up for takeoff as the powerful engine had a lot of torque and tried to twist the plane counter clockwise. Frieda would have to apply enough right rudder and right aileron control to keep the plane straight on takeoff. Other than that it was similar to the 108 and a lot faster. She was thankful for Al's excellent tutoring and his persistence about her being very good at instrument flying because in this very fast plane there is practically no time for error. You have to trust the instruments and act accordingly. Every day before the Big Race she was at the Club putting in time on the 109. She even did a run down to Marseille and back, checking for land marks and high altitude wind current. She noted there was one heading east at 4,300 meters when about half way back from Marseille.

One rainy day she couldn't fly because Peter had the plane painted with his advertising making it look more like a commercial sport plane than a fighter plane. She was thankful to him because he was the spark plug that created this situation--now all she had to do was win the race.

On the day of the race, June 12, 1936, it was slightly cloudy, with a west wind, a perfect day for a race. There were ten contestants: from England, USA, France, Canada, Italy and Romania, with most of them from the USA. They all had very fast planes. Frieda knew by looking at the types of planes and by having read about these famous women pilots that it was not going to be an easily won race.

On the day before the race, like at the Club Race, they drew for their takeoff positions. She drew number 8 and a big figure eight was sprayed on the sides of the plane's fuselage. Peter nearly had a fit when they tried to spray over his logo.

The first plane took off at nine AM, then every fifteen minutes they took off in order of their draw number, with their takeoff time being recorded. The procedure was to fly to the Marseille Airport, cross over a finish line, with their time being recorded. The pilots were all booked into a hotel in Marseille where they would rest for the night. The next day they all had to be at the Marseille terminal before 9 AM. They were given signed slips indicating their recorded arrival at the finish line in Marseille. Then they again took off in the order of their original number. Frieda was pleased to note that she had passed several other planes on the leg to Marseille. Also a few entries had mechanical problems, which eliminated them from the race. Frieda thought that she was glad she didn't race the engine too hard on the first leg; she was going to save the engine until the last half hour of the race.

On the way down from Berlin she used a course she had plotted on the trial run she did before the race. It went Berlin to Frankfurt to Marseille and she had recorded her times on each leg coming down so she would have an idea of how she was doing coming back. Her return time was just slightly ahead when she reached Frankfurt. When she turned east on the Berlin leg, Frieda climbed steadily up to 4,500 meters then cruised at that altitude until she was just past Magdeburg, then she started her long high powered descent to the finish line. When she was about eight kilometers from the finish line she could see two planes below and just ahead of her. She was gaining on them very fast and she passed the first one, a Dehavilland twin engine Comet flown by the Canadian, Rollie Moore, about a kilometre from the finish line and the other flown by the American, Jaqueline Cochran. She roared past them with engine smoking and revved a way over the red line, about two seconds before the finish line. She wasn't sure who she was passing at the last second, but she wasn't going to ease up until her plane screamed over the finish line. She managed to keep the motor running as she banked, turned back and landed with an engine belching smoke.

As soon as she stopped, a fire truck roared up to the plane and sprayed foam all over the engine cowling. After Frieda leaped onto the ground the plane was towed away from the other planes, in case it was going to explode. Frieda started to run towards the Club House, someone grabbed her, then she realized it was Al. Even though she was tired and exhausted, she appreciated the hug and kiss he gave her.

The next day the winners were declared. Frieda had won the first prize purse of one hundred thousand marks. While being presented the Lufthansa Trophy by Adolph Hitler, he remarked quietly to her with a smile, "I hope you go easier on our Transport planes."

That night Frieda, Al and Peter, along with his wife, all celebrated at the Grand Hotel in Berlin having champagne cocktails, dinner and dancing. The orchestra leader announced, "The next dance is in honour of Frau Frieda Schmidt, the world's fastest woman aviatrix who has just broken the world speed record for land planes." The spotlight was put on her and Al as they danced. The crowd gave her a big round of applause.

When they sat down Frieda said, "OK, when?"

"I'm putting in the application tomorrow."

"I don't mean that, you silly bugger."

"Careful, I'm going to be your boss, OH! You mean the marriage. Gee, I don't know about that, you're kind of fast for me."

Three days after the race, Al brought Frieda into the Lufthansa office and had her sign all the appropriate papers to be hired as a pilot on Lufthansa. He then took her into the Chief Pilot's office and introduced them. Al couldn't help thinking that while Frieda was being instructed by the Head of the Pilots in the firm, that it wouldn't have been this easy for her when she first got her commercial ticket. Al was pleased they had waited until Frieda had become famous; it would make for a better relationship for her with her fellow workers and his job a little less political.

Third Officer Frieda Schmidt was assigned to fly on one of the local flights as a probation pilot acting as co-pilot flying a JU 52 Tri-motor Junker. For safety reasons and passenger comfort all local flights were done in the daytime. This meant Frieda was home each night. Al was still living in his own apartment as he was waiting until they were married to finally move in with Frieda.

Chapter 4

IN NOVEMBER 1936, Frieda was promoted to full pilot rating, also she was assigned to be second officer on the Giant Junker JU G38, that flew on the Berlin to Paris to London flight. It had a crew of seven and carried thirty-four passengers plus cargo; it made two round trips per day. All the crew were senior employees as this was the Flagship of the Fleet. Frieda flew on the JU G38 until August 1937 when Lufthansa received the first of six Heinkel Transports and Frieda was taken off the JU G38 to be checked out on the Heinkel. In September 1937 Frieda Schmidt was promoted to First Officer and became a Captain flying the Heinkels.

In November 1937 Al chose Frieda to be his pilot to fly a Heinkel on an inspection trip of the West African Lufthansa Air Stations. Al would act as co-pilot as she was qualified on the Heinkel and he wasn't. They used the same route as they did in 1935. Only this time he was the one receiving the instructions about the plane they were flying in.

They stayed at the same hotels in Toulouse and Casablanca and enjoyed it even more than the first time. Before leaving Berlin Al had wired Em asking if it was okay with Em to come on a certain date in November. Em wired back, "Welcome OK Em."

They didn't have to land at El Aaiun because this particular plane was equipped with special long-range petrol tanks and was used on the African long-range flights.

During the flight Al kept himself busy studying the contracts and specifications for the construction of the new station at Rinsque. He wanted to be able to carry out a quick and proper inspection before going to the Palace.

They landed at the new Lufthansa facility in Rinsque. They both did an inspection tour and checked everything out. The facility was built properly and complied with the specifications and drawings as laid out in the contract that Al carried in his briefcase. He was pleased with the way the contractor, Mr. Andersen, had done a good job without any complications. The station supervisor delivered them to Em's palace in the Company's service truck, along with their luggage.

Em gave them a warm greeting at the palace door, and then he led them out to the terrace where a very attractive lady was sitting. Em said, "Frieda – Al, I'd like you to meet my friend and companion Marie Rochelle."

Em didn't say wife, so obviously this was his girlfriend - companion, the same as Frieda and Al. (Al noticed Em called him Al because that was how Al signed the telegram.)

Right away Frieda and Marie took a liking to each other. After dinner they were having gin cocktails out on the terrace. Al held his glass up looking at it and to Em, he said, with a quizzical twist of his head, "Gin cocktail?"

Em laughed, "Al, you don't think that I went to all those institutes of learning without learning how to drink? As a matter of fact that's how I met Marie in Paris. No, I wasn't drunk--we were at a party. Marie hadn't married yet, she became widowed down here. Her husband, a good friend of mine, was killed in a mining accident, and we had all met at that infamous party in Paris."

"By the way Frieda, I see by the papers you are a famous aviatrix. Did you do any flying on the way down?" He gave that sly wink of his.

"Yes Em, I certainly did. As a matter of fact I was instructing Al on this trip. By the way, do you remember what I said last time?"

"Yes, I believe it was something about learning to fly first."

"Well?"

Frieda answered, "I don't know what he is waiting for. Maybe he's hoping someone will steal me, then he can get out of marrying me."

They were all sitting there grinning at Al.

He was just smiling, then he reached into his jacket pocket and pulled out a velvet-coated box, opened it up, displaying a one carat engagement ring and a gold wedding band. As he held it out to Frieda he said, "Will you marry me, Frieda Schmidt?"

There was a dead silence until she got up, leaned over, kissed him and said, "Yes, Albert Wirth. I shall marry you."

Em and Marie were clapping and wiping the tears from their faces. Em called for the servant to bring out a bottle of chilled champagne, then they all toasted to the happy occasion.

Em said, "The wedding shall be held here. I'll prepare a guest list and arrange for the marriage ceremony and the reception. This palace is long overdue for a good party."

Em asked if they had any preference for religion and they both replied, "No, any padre would do as long as he signs the wedding certificate making them legal."

Frieda looking at Al said, "How long have you had that wedding certificate?"

"I got it the day before the big race. It didn't matter to me whether you won or lost as long as you weren't hurt or injured doing it."

They had a really happy celebration that night and both Frieda and Al were glad they were going to be married here with their friends in this romantic setting.

The next day Marie had the chauffeur drive the two women to Dakar to do the shopping for Frieda's wedding apparel. Marie picked out the wedding gown and she insisted on paying for it as her present to Frieda.

She said, "Look Frieda, you are a famous person and there is going to be royalty and a lot of wealthy persons attending. You have to look like a beautiful princess, which you are, so let's do it up right." She even picked an elegant evening dress for Frieda, knowing she would need it for the formal occasions she would be attending here and in Berlin.

Al had brought his Lufthansa Captain's uniform, complete with sash and sword from his days as a Captain in the German Air Force.

The wedding was set to be on the Saturday two days hence. Em knew a rebel priest who had broken away from the Church and was doing his own thing, like getting married and other rebellious acts. He agreed to perform the service as long as he could bring the native princess he married and enjoy the reception party. Besides, for years he had been hoping to see inside the palace someday—it was no problem.

The wedding was performed out in the palace garden on the lawn surrounded by palm trees and fragrant flowers. There were seats for eighty guests with a violinist and a harp player rendering pleasant music for the congregation.

Al was standing with a friend of Em's, Karl Andersen as his best man, in front of the parson. At a signal from the minister the musicians struck up the wedding song. Em, with Frieda on his arm, strolled up to the wedding line with Marie as the bride's maid of honour. It was a formal affair and the consensual attire of the guests displayed that.

It was a brief but respectable service. When the musicians struck up the Wedding March every one stood and clapped, then followed the wedding party into the palace ballroom, which had been set for a large sit down dinner, followed by a celebration party with a live orchestra and dancing. After Frieda and Al had their wedding waltz during the party, Em approached Karl and Al who were standing off to one side.

He said, "By the way, you two haven't formally met. Karl is the contractor that built your Lufthansa Station here in Rinsque."

Em said, "Can you two meet here with me Monday morning at ten o'clock?" When they confirmed, he said with a smile, "OK, no more business, let's have a party."

Recovering from the party, Sunday was spent relaxing and discussing about the guests and the wedding gifts received.

On Monday morning Marie, who was also a guest of Em's, took Frieda shopping in Dakar while the men were going to do their business once again.

Chapter 5

EM EXPLAINED TO Karl that Al was the President and CEO of Lufthansa, and then he explained to Al that Karl was the representative for an Eastern Oil company. He suggested that there was an opportunity here for all three to start up a petrol supply company to service airplanes and ships. They had an in depth discussion as to what the market is, where to set up the facilities, how to finance it and how do they go about setting up a company.

Before the day was over they had decided to form a company, and what to call it. They agreed that the name should be REAAFCO (Rinsque-Em-Al-Andersen-Fuel Company). Al's part will be to set up a Lufthansa fuel depot here at their station. It would require installing a pumping station at a ship dock to storage tanks that will supply aircraft and ships both here and at Dakar and other stations up the coast of Africa.

It was agreed that each would have a one third partnership in the company and it should have its registered office in Switzerland with a Swiss account number.

Em had a lawyer friend in Switzerland who he'll pay to register the company. Em will act as manager and see to it that the customers pay their accounts and the funds are deposited in the Swiss account.

When flying back to Casablanca, Frieda quizzed Al about the meeting he had with Em and Karl.

"Karl is in the oil and petrol business. I was making arrangements for Lufthansa to get its petrol here in West Africa."

Al didn't want Frieda involved because she was an employee of Lufthansa and this was a private matter that had to be kept confidential. The fewer that know about it the better, especially with that Gestapo man, Heinrich Himmler, snooping around spying on everyone. It'll be safer for Frieda if she doesn't know anything about the partnership company, he thought.

Frieda did most of the flying and brought Al up to date on flying the Heinkel. She handled the plane expertly with complete confidence, even in the rough weather locations and in navigating dead-on to their destinations. He was very proud of her and wouldn't mind being her co-pilot on the Lufthansa flights.

They both considered the return flight to be their honeymoon trip and enjoyed it as much as the first trip they took to Africa.

The day they arrived back in Berlin, Al had his things moved to Frieda's apartment. That night she cooked a roast beef dinner and they celebrated with a bottle of good German white wine and finally slept as a married couple with no guilty conscience.

They noticed the manager observing them so Al explained to him about the marriage in Africa, knowing that the rumour mill would spread gossip about them.

With Frieda being a celebrity, it didn't take long before the reporters were after them to put their picture and story of the wedding in the papers. Al went along with it for publicity reasons as the airline could use some good PR, especially about Frieda being a celebrated pilot and a full captain for flying the Heinkel all over Europe and Africa.

Lufthansa was enjoying a considerable increase in their passenger flights. Al realized the company would have to obtain larger and faster planes to handle the future growth; he started to get specs of planes from all over Europe and the USA. The American Locheed 14 that Imperial Airways was using was fast but not large enough to handle the increase in usage. The Douglas DC3 was a very good craft, but again, Al was looking for something larger.

Just about that time, July 1937, there was an Aircraft Exhibition in Paris put on by the manufacturers of transport planes. This was just what Al needed--a place to see all the planes get their specs and talk to the company reps.

The one company that had a plane that intrigued Al was the Focke Wulf Company here in Germany. The one they displayed was a large four-engine transport that carried 26 passengers and had a very long range of 4,400 km, using the reliable BMW radial engine, which had a good service and maintenance record.

Al talked with the General Manager and designer of this transport, Herr Kurt Tank who asked Kurt to visit Al at the Lufthansa Office and bring all the specs and information about this plane so that Al could present a proposal to the Directors of Lufthansa about purchasing this plane that the Focke Wulf Co. named the "FW200 Condor."

When Al made his report to Hitler upon his return from Paris, he mentioned the Focke Wulf Condor.

Hitler said, "Ah yes, the Focke Wulf Company. They have supplied Herman with several flying boats. Good company. Will this Condor fly the entirety of the Atlantic to the USA or South America nonstop?"

"Yes, no problem. Also, it is just the plane to carry a payload that'll make such trips profitable. Do you recommend we purchase some of these planes when funds are available?"

"Yes, by all means. You are the head of Lufthansa, it is your decision to make. If you feel the company should have the plane, then buy it."

After Al left Hitler's office he thought to himself, he wants me to get the plane, but it is obvious he doesn't want to appear to be involved with the purchase of this long-range plane. He thought back to their original conversations when the questions were always about flying the Atlantic Ocean. Gradually the puzzle was starting to fall into place and Al had a suspicion about it. He felt something was going to happen soon that would confirm his thinking.

Al put the proposition to the Board of Directors after presenting a projection of the Company's payloads and the demand for larger and faster aircraft. It was obvious, in order to keep up to the demand and to compete with the other Airlines, that they have to upgrade their fleet. Peter put forth the motion to purchase four Focke Wulf Condors. The motion was passed.

When the financial report was presented to the Board, included was a statement of what the airline was paying for fuel per litre, along with a comparison sheet showing what it had paid in previous years. When the company comptroller first presented the comparison sheet Al was concerned it might reveal something about his involvement in the fuel business. At the Board meeting one of the directors mentioned that it was strange the cost of fuel has dropped since getting rid of that pompous Director and maybe he had a way of skimming a kickback from the suppliers. He also mentioned that it was a good thing Chairman Al got rid of him and his relatives.

Chapter 6

ON JUNE 15, 1938, the first Condor was delivered to Lufthansa. The Focke Wulf Chief Test Pilot Kurt Tank and designer of the Condor took Al, Frieda, Lufthansa's Chief of Pilots and two of Lufthansa's senior pilots, for a check out flight. They all took turns handling the plane and all were very pleased with its performance. It was assigned to one of the long distance flights, which was a money maker. Frieda had to wait her turn to get one of the other three Condors, however, she was in no hurry because she was satisfied with the local runs being able to be home each night.

When the fourth Condor was delivered in October of '38, Al decided he should take it to South America to check out the facilities available for servicing Lufthansa transport planes. He had been talking previously to Air France and Portuguese pilots about landing fields and service facilities in South America. Evidently Pan American Airlines established servicing airports all the way down into Argentina and were willing to lease space and service to European airlines in order to collect revenue from them.

In his next report to Hitler he quizzed Hitler whether he should make a survey flight to Argentina with one of the Condors. He wasn't surprised at Hitler's enthusiasm about the idea.

"Yes, I think that is an excellent suggestion and I think it should be done as soon as possible before other airlines get in ahead of you. I think you should use Frieda as your pilot--she'll probably be one of the pilots eventually on that run."

The willingness to support the flight didn't surprise Al but the suggestion to use Frieda did. What had Hitler got up his sleeve?

Condor Number 4 was held back from Flight Schedule. Both Frieda and Al did a lot of flight-testing of No.4, both doing their checkout on the plane.

Al contacted Pan Am and got the OK to use their facilities in South America. Al had planned the South American flight to coincide with their anniversary in November. He wired Em advising him about when they will arrive in Rinsque.

Frieda was very pleased that she was going to be one of the pilots during the flight and have the opportunity to visit with her friends in Rinsque again.

The Condor was able to fly direct to Algiers from Berlin. She plotted the same course she used for the big race to Marseille and then across the Mediterranean to Algiers. This plane was a real pleasure to fly with its automatic pilot, directional radio compass and other aids for flight, even a galley for having meals in flight.

One of the most noticeable features was the pressurized cabin, making it possible to fly over the stormy weather, consequently offering a smoother and more comfortable flight. What a difference to the original transports! Both Al and Frieda agreed this plane is going to do a lot for Lufthansa. Also the flight time is going to be less because this plane is twice as fast as the older planes. Also, a much longer flight range means fewer landings and less cost for the long hops as it was much more fuel efficient.

They stayed the first night in Algiers; again this was all new to Frieda. They had the plane refueled, put some supplies in the galley and made ready for an early flight the next morning. Like in

Casablanca, here in Algiers there was a comfortable breeze coming off the sea making it nice to enjoy their meal in the dining room with some belly dancing and music entertainment.

The next morning they thoroughly checked out the plane then took off for El Aaiun.

The airfield at El Aaiun had been moved to a better location outside the town. It was now long enough to handle the bigger planes. Also like Algiers, there happened to be a refueling station that was owned by a company called REAAFCO--this was their next destination after Algiers, for refueling. They were both pleased with the bigger landing strip and the up to date service facilities. Frieda taxied the Condor right up to the service tarmac for fuelling. As soon as they finished getting their fuel they did the pre-flight checklist, then took off for Rinsque.

They landed in Rinsque at five PM and went directly to the Palace to have a relaxing time before dinner with Em and Marie. It was nice to be in the tropics in November as the night was warm and pleasant with flowers scenting the air as they sat out on the terrace having a cocktail before dinner. Marie and Frieda were busy catching up on the latest gossip and news about each other. Em took Al to one side before dinner and told Al he'd like to bring him up to date on the happenings and progress of REAAFCO.

After dinner Em and Al went into Em's office. When Al was comfortably seated, Em presented him with a Profit and Loss Statement which showed that the company had made a considerable profit and showed how much was put into each of the partner's Swiss accounts. Al was stunned. He didn't have a clue there could be so much income from the operation.

Em was studying him when Al read the statement, then he just smiled and said, "Al, I don't think we have seen the real potential here. I have a feeling it is going to get a lot bigger." They discussed the future and possible expansions of the business. Em asked Al about the political situation in Germany.

Al hesitated with a concerned look on his face. "It doesn't look good, the Gestapo is throwing people into jail for the smallest reason. They are using terror tactics to control the citizens. I'm afraid we're going to be going into a war any day now."

"Al, if you and Frieda want to get out of there, you both could come to Rinsque to live. You'd have an income from the Company and could live quite comfortably. I suggest when you are ready to defect, send me a telegram that your aunt died so your visit is postponed. You could take one of the smaller planes of Lufthansa and destroy it in a simulated crash. I could report to Lufthansa that you both were killed in the crash. There would be no reason for them to look for both of you or the plane."

"Wow! Em you should have been a mystery writer. I'll keep your suggestion in mind and I sure appreciate your friendship and support and I want to thank you for helping us with the marriage and of course including me in on a wonderful business adventure."

Em laughed when Al mentioned about mystery writing. "When I was at the university in Paris I had to write stories as part of my language course. I found I liked writing mysteries and got my best marks writing them."

"I do feel that war is going to be declared within a year or so. Of course, Italy has been waging war in Africa ever since the Spanish Revolution has let up. Even here in this part of Africa we could be affected--I hope not."

"Where are you headed for on this trip, Al?"

"I'm planning to set up service facilities in Brazil and Argentina for Lufthansa so when we set up scheduled runs to South America, we will be prepared."

"Did Adolph Hitler suggest this plan?"

"Yes, actually it was he who started the plan going in 1935 by his conversations and questions. Why?"

"Well, it struck me that it is strange to be planning the extension of Lufthansa into South America if he is going to start war in the near future."

Al was smiling at Em. "Just between us, I've had the same thought for some time, and I am sure that is why he had me set up the depot here in Africa ready to go across the Atlantic to South America. It is quite obvious that I am part of his plan; I can't divulge my thoughts on it right now, but I'm sure he needs me and I have to play along with it for Frieda's and my protection."

Em smiled and said he agreed with Al and that Al had better not discuss his thoughts with anyone else—even Frieda for their safety. Remember to send that telegram when necessary, he added.

It was a very enjoyable visit with Marie and Em. Marie was especially intrigued with Frieda's experience flying the different big transport planes to different parts of Europe and now flying this big transport to South America and down to Buenos Aires.

Em and Marie went to the airfield to see them off. Al and Frieda did a thorough check of the plane, and then while Frieda was warming up the engines, Em pointed out to Al the facilities that had been installed by REAAFCO. Then Al took Em and Marie into the plane so they could all say good-bye together. They all gathered on the flight deck so Em and Marie could wish them "Bon Voyage" and as good friends they hugged each other and said their goodbyes.

After Em and Marie departed from the plane, Frieda taxied the plane out to the takeoff point on the airstrip. She gunned the engines and the plane roared down the strip for the takeoff. The plane lifted off quickly because it was not heavily loaded with only two persons aboard, even though it was carrying a full load of fuel. Frieda took off heading west and when they were up about two hundred meters she circled back over the Rinsque Airport, she did a little wing waggle as a bon voyage salute to Em and Marie. She then headed the plane for Brazil, South America.

Chapter 7

THEIR DESTINATION IN Brazil was Recife where Pan American had its service facilities. It took twelve hours to make the trip. Frieda was glad to have Al take over several times, even though the plane had an automatic pilot. They had sandwiches for lunch and supper and took turns using the washroom facilities which was a luxury compared to the facilities on the older transports. It was dark when they did a check run around the airport. Al had wired the Pan Am office two days earlier advising them of their approximate ETA (estimated time of arrival). After several minutes of buzzing over the airfield, Al and Frieda began to wonder if they were going to have to do a guessing game of trying to land with using only the plane's landing lights which could be done, but was very risky and only done when there is no other choice. Finally the field lights were turned on lighting up the runway. Al previously had received from Pan Am the airport layout and the high points around the field such as trees and buildings. They did a careful approach and landed safely in South America. Al asked the airport attendant how come it took so long to turn on the lights. The attendant told him that he lived about a kilometer from the field and the Pan Am pilots usually fly over his house as a signal for him to turn on the lights. Al asked him to point out where he lived so that they could buzz his place next time. They used the overnight accommodations supplied by Pan Am and went to bed tired but happy to be here. The Pan Am crew took over to service the plane as soon as they departed it. They wanted to be ready to leave early the next morning for the long flight to Rio de Janeiro.

The approach to Rio was spectacular; they both were excited and exhilarated about seeing Rio de Janeiro for the first time. Al told a pleased Frieda that they would have to stay for at least two days while he made the arrangements for Lufthansa's landing and service facilities.

After clearing the Brazilian Customs they went to the Pan Am office at the Airport. Al gave his card to the secretary telling her that the manager expected him. They were led into the manager's office where the manager, Jan O'Hagan, greeted them. Al introduced Frieda as his wife, Frieda Schmidt.

Jan said, "Ah yes, the famous racing aviatrix. Welcome to Rio de Janeiro. Please be seated. Have either of you been to Rio de Janeiro before?"

When they both stated no, Jan said, "Great, when you get settled at the hotel give me a phone call, I'll have you picked up. You are both to be my guests at the Club Cocabaña, for dinner and dancing. By the way, all arrangements have been made for handling the plane's servicing. All the pilots have to do is sign for the service--everything is arranged with the banks for the draft transfers, so relax and enjoy Rio."

Two very happy people headed by taxi to their hotel.

"I noticed you introduced me as Frieda Schmidt. Why is that?"

"Well, if I just introduced you as my wife, do you think he would've been impressed, as much as he was, when he realized who you were? You know, honey, you are famous, especially in the aviation world."

They had a very enjoyable night, dining and dancing in this famous club with its marble dance floor and its big band playing Latin rhythms. The Latins are very fond of and enjoy dancing. Jan taught Frieda the samba and Jan's wife Rita showed Al how to dance it. Even though they were a little tired they had a wonderful evening being entertained by these vibrant people.

The next day they took a tour and rested up while enjoying this exotic city, and they prepared to leave early the next morning.

The flight to Buenos Aires is the same distance as Rio to Recife so it also took about five hours of enjoyable scenery.

After getting through the Argentine Customs, they went into the Pan Am office. Evidently the Rio Manager had phoned down and advised the Buenos Aires Manager of their coming. They were sent in directly to his office and just as the Rio Manager did, they were dined and entertained as important customers. This manager has also made all the arrangements for handling Lufthansa. It was a lot easier than Al had expected. Of course having a famous person as the Lufthansa pilot sure helped. Al had kept a diary of everything and the names of all the people along with notes of their conversations. He was sure Hitler was going to be very interested in this trip so he had better give a very good report of the whole trip in South America.

On the three-day flight back to Rinsque he kept going over his notes. He had to memorize everything and not leave any notes around for the Gestapo to find.

Em was very glad to see them back. He suggested they have a meeting with Karl and then all three shareholders could inspect their holdings in Dakar and Rinsque. After inspecting the facilities they decided to have a meeting to discuss their future plans.

They had their meeting in Em's office at the Palace. Karl presented them with sheets showing the locations of their fuelling stations. They were at Dakar, Rinsque, Aaiun and were in the middle of building one at Casablanca. Karl mentioned that the French have the toe hold in Algiers and some of the other North Africa locations. He said he wasn't concerned about trying to get places in the Mediterranean area. He suggested that if there were a war in the making, which looked very likely at present, the Mediterranean ports would be very hard to service.

He turned to Al and said: "Al, I know it is not fair to put this question to you, but we have to know. Do you think that war is imminent in Europe?"

"Yes, to be honest with you, it can break out within the next year. Do you think it will close down our business?"

"Not at first, but the whole of Europe is going to need fuel for their war machines. Eventually we could become very rich supplying ships and aircraft. Or we could be caught in the middle of it and be wiped out. Our method of using Swiss banking could be very convenient for us in supplying all sides in a war. It has happened before."

After Karl left, Al and Em were discussing things about the business.

"Do you really think Al, that there is going to be a war soon?"

"Yes Em, just between you and me, I know that there is going to be a war soon. I'm too close to it to not see it. I feel it is going to happen next year. I have a feeling we'll be seeing each other eventually in very unusual circumstances, and I hope it will a pleasant reunion. Do you trust Karl?"

"Well Al, let me put it this way. I've known Karl for many years and I have trusted him on other business dealings. But no business should rely entirely on trust; when it comes to money every man has a price. In our case it is a matter of each one of us needing the other, a three link chain. We need Lufthansa and you need Karl, yes and both of you need me to be the 'go between.' I also have a feeling that this is going to be a beautiful, rich friendship. Everything we have discussed is strictly confidential, for the sake of the business and our own safety."

The next morning Frieda and Al took off after a somber saying of goodbyes and assurances of keeping in touch.

They followed the same route back to Berlin, enjoying every minute flying this wonderful, new and comfortable transport.

Albert spent most of his time going over what he was going to report to Hitler. He felt the Fuhrer was going to ask a million questions about South America and the trip. Al had to be careful not to let it slip out about REAAFCO.

Both Frieda and Al had to rest the day after landing back in Berlin before going back to work. It was quite a letdown for Frieda to go back to flying the Heinkels after flying the Condor, but she knew that it would not be very long before she'll be on the Condors.

Al wasn't surprised at Hitler's enthusiasm about the trip. He asked about the fuel stops, their accommodations, the arrangements for servicing the plane, whether the people were friendly, and was the plane comfortable to fly in.

The Condor was very popular with the flying public; there was such a demand to fly in the Condor that Lufthansa was forced to order two more. In his report to Hitler Al told him that he had ordered two more Condors and that he was thinking of storing one in the spare hangar at the Berlin Flying Club. Hitler asked him why he was placing the Condor in storage. Al explained the plane was to be held as a standby, to be used as a backup in case of an emergency, or a breakdown of one of the other Condors in their fleet. Also. Al explained it was to be used as Hitler's private plane. Hitler appeared quite pleased about the idea of having a Condor for his private use. He told Al that he was going to have it named The Immellman II, after the famous German Ace in World War I. The way he quizzed Al about the trip and the plane made Al think, "Yes, another piece to the puzzle. Does Hitler think I am on to his plan, whatever it is, or is he just toying with me?"

The day after the Condor was placed in the Club Hangar, Al went to inspect the plane and the facilities. The security man on duty told Al that some Gestapo men came around that morning, asking all sorts of questions about why the plane was stored there. They insisted on inspecting the plane, which he let them do, because he didn't want to get in trouble with them. Al told him he did the right thing and then he asked the security man if they asked by whose authority the plane was stored there. When the man said no, Al realized that only two people had known the plane was here, Hitler and himself. Al went straight to Hitler's office but before going in he had printed a large note saying, "I think there is a listening device in your office." When he entered he put his finger to his lips and put the note on Hitler's desk. He then went behind Hitler and turned on the radio that was on a small table behind the desk. He tuned it to a music station and then said, "I have reason to believe there is a listening device in here."

He then explained what had happened at the Club with the Condor. Hitler was sitting at his desk bug eyed, becoming red in the face and starting to get mad. Al again put his finger to his lips and said, "Leave it with me. I'll try to figure out some way to set a trap."

That night Al and Frieda went to a restaurant for dinner and during the meal he explained what had happened that day. They discussed the possibility of a device in their own apartment. Frieda said, "If there is, I think I know how to find out. I'll show you tonight when we get in bed. They are going to hear the sexiest love making ever made in Berlin." Frieda made the wildest sex noises one could ever imagine. If it was a man listening, he was going to get an earful of a woman putting on a great act of enjoying sex.

Two days later as Al entered his office, his secretary and one from another office were reading the newspaper and laughing. When Al asked what was so funny, his secretary said there is piece in the paper about a man that is being charged by the police because he beat up his wife for not giving him good sex. They were laughing because she knew him. Al asked her what he does for a living and she said he used to do radio repair work but she thought he had some kind of government job now.

Al reported his finding to Hitler. All his reporting was done now with the radio playing as though there was no one in Hitler's office and he was just listening to the music. Hitler suggested that Al give him hand written reports that he would burn immediately after reading. Also he was to carry on a non committal conversation to avoid suspicion by the listener. Al is almost dead sure now that he is somehow tied in with Hitler in a plan of some kind. Time will tell.

Chapter 8

IN JULY 1939 Hitler promoted Al to Minister of Air Transportation. His portfolio description stated that the Minister is responsible for the acquisition and supply of aircraft transportation for all German government requirements. It didn't take long for Al to realize his main job was to co-ordinate the transportation of military personnel and supplies for a sudden expansion of the German Army. What was supposed to have been a non-active Reserve Force had been mobilized into an active army and was invading Czechoslovakia, Austria and Hungary. The Gestapo had previously infiltrated the governments of these countries, and then moved the military arm, the Black Shirts, into these countries and, by forceful means, cleared the path for the invasion of the Army.

The different divisions of the invaders requested the use of air transport to ship supplies and personnel. It was the Ministry's job to dispatch the planes in the most convenient and expedient method.

Lufthansa was made redundant; its planes were all transferred to the Department of Air Transport Ministry. Peter Wasmuth was appointed Deputy Minister to Albert Wirth and all the Lufthansa personnel were transferred to the ATM.

The requirements of the invasions were so vast that the planes on hand couldn't keep up to the demand. Al was having trouble getting more transport planes. The one he wanted was the old workhorse of aviation the JU 52 tri-motor; it was the best suited for the type of jobs they were doing. There was one hitch in trying to get this airplane--it was also in demand by the Army and by Goering as a paratrooper plane. When Al complained to Hitler about his problem, he was surprised at Hitler's solution. Hitler made Al a General, giving Al more power to be able to order the planes he needed. As well as a General he was still the Minister in charge of Air Transport, giving him two swords to fight with, a very powerful position. He continued to make direct reports to Hitler.

Frieda, being one of the Lufthansa pilots, was transferred to the ATM. The demand for pilots was as critical as the aircraft shortage. When making one of his reports to Hitler, Al suggested that women be recruited and trained as transport and ferrying pilots to fill in the need for pilots. Again, Hitler second guessed Al.

He said, "That is an excellent suggestion and to make it work properly make Frieda the head of the training program. I'll make her a Colonel in charge of the Women's Auxiliary Air Force. She'll be in charge of all female pilot training and it is to be under your command."

Al got Peter to give him a hand in helping Frieda prepare a training program for women pilots. They used one that was similar to the one used by the Berlin Flying Club, that is, starting with gliders then gradually working up to transports and military aircraft.

At one of the report meetings with Hitler, Al suggested maybe they should use the Condor that was stored at the Flying Club as part of the Air Transport usage. Actually he was testing Hitler to see what he would say. Hitler's face showed concern and he rejected the idea without giving a reason why.

Evidently, the suggestion to use the stored Condor started Hitler thinking about that plane because several times during later meetings between them, Hitler would quiz Al about the condition of the Condor. One time he asked what colour was the plane? Al said it was natural aluminum like all the other planes in the Lufthansa fleet. Then Hitler did something unusual: he switched off the radio, then in a normal voice as if Al had just come into his office, he said, "That Condor plane that is stored at the Flying Club. I'm going to have it painted white and put a big red cross on it. When the right time comes I'll use it to bomb New York, USA, if they come into a war against Germany. It will reach New York nonstop from Germany, won't it?"

"Yes, no problem, it can reach New York easily and especially disguised as a Red Cross Plane." Al thought, that ought to throw whoever is enquiring about the Condor off the scent. It had certainly thrown him off its intended use, but he still had a feeling about where he and Frieda fit into Hitler's plan.

In September 1939 Germany invaded Poland. This was against the agreement Hitler had made with France and Britain assuring them that he would not do so. The United Kingdom and France declared war against Germany immediately. It was too late. Germany had been building a Navy, Army and Air Force for several years right under their noses. Hitler had gained control over half of Europe. In a very short time he utilized the Blitzkrieg method of warfare, working his way through France, Denmark and Norway.

Al was busier than a one-armed paper hanger trying to keep up to the demand for air transport. There were supplies, equipment, personnel and wounded to be hauled by air. This was a far cry from the scheduled flight days of Lufthansa. Pilots and planes were being worked to the limit.

Frieda was using the old Berlin Flying Club facilities for her training quarters. At first, there were twenty per month graduating as qualified pilots, ten for transport and ten for military planes. By the beginning of 1940, there was such a loss of military aircraft it was necessary for the women pilots to be qualified to fly any military plane so they could ferry the planes from the factories to the front lines; the graduation at the women's training centre had risen to 50 per month.

Frieda had selected highly qualified pilots as instructors; some of the originals were members of the Berlin Flying Club. Gradually the number of instructors grew. There were casualties from training accidents and losses by pilot error and the odd few by attack from enemy fighters near the front lines. To encourage enlistment in the Women's Auxiliary Air force, the graduates were given a very smart uniform and this helped in the recruiting but didn't cut down their loss percentage. It was very heart breaking for Frieda to have to make and send letters of condolence to their parents or loved ones. She purposely avoided getting to know any of them and would only preside as the commanding officer at the graduation ceremony.

By 1941 the fighting had spread into North Africa, the front lines stretching from Africa to the north of Norway. Al's ATM and Frieda's WAF were working to their limit. They were both very busy and didn't see each other often enough. Whenever they got a chance, they would go to the senior officers' club in Berlin. Frieda, in her smart uniform, was very striking and several times had to ward off advances from other senior officers even though she was sitting with a very handsome general, Al.

When Al was making one of his reports to Hitler, the question of petrol supply came up. Al told Hitler that he had been transporting fuel from Romania using JU52s that have been modified into cargo planes to haul drums of fuel to wherever they were needed. Hitler asked Al if he had any connections in North Africa because the forces there had been requesting more fuel. Al said he would look into his records and see what he could find.

Al contacted the German Embassy in Madrid by special security code to see if they could arrange with a fuel supply company named REAAFCO in Rinsque and if they could arrange to supply fuel at Casablanca to be picked up by JU52 tanker planes. Al received confirmation in three days; immediately he dispatched four of the special cargo planes off the Romanian run to Casablanca and they were to load up then fly their load to a little place in Tunisia called Remada where the German forces had a supply station.

Al found out from the Comptroller General later on that the REAAFCO Company was stupid. It requested all payments to be made to a Swiss account in Swiss francs. Didn't they know that Germany was going to win the war?

At the next meeting with Hitler he congratulated Al on the good job of getting fuel to the places that needed it. He had the radio playing so they could talk freely, and he asked Al how he arranged to get the fuel in Africa. Does he know the Company and will Lufthansa be able to get fuel from them when the war is over? Al, in trying to read what Hitler had on his mind, assured him that the fuel would be available when needed.

The United States of America entered the war in December of 1941. It was a great blow to Germany because with its might in manufacturing it could turn the tide of advantage against Germany especially since the treaty between Russia and Germany had collapsed. Russia started to receive arms from the USA as did Britain. The big blow came when Rommel was defeated in North Africa and the American Forces landed in there.

The Americans established Dakar as one of their landing fields in Africa where there was a company ready to supply all the fuel they needed and they just had to pay in US dollars to a Swiss bank account. As a matter of fact, this same company, called REAAFCO, supplied *all* their fuel in Africa. It was very convenient.

One night when Al and Frieda were lying in bed with the radio playing they were discussing the set back in the war and their future. She looked at him and said, "Aren't you concerned about our future? Things are not going well for Germany and you don't appear to be too upset. Maybe you're glad the war might be over soon."

He turned the radio up a little higher because he still didn't trust that snake Himmler. He replied, "Yes, Frieda, I'm hoping the war will end soon, but I have the strangest feeling that there is something in the way of a great life for us in the near future. By the way I have bought a little farm out past the Flying Club field just as a precaution against bombing raids on Berlin."

Al was almost hoping the war would carry on a lot longer than expected. Every day it continued, they were becoming richer through their interest in REAAFCO.

Hitler made a big mistake in attacking Russia instead of conquering Britain like he could have. The war on the Russian front had stepped up considerably with supplies and equipment being supplied by the USA. Frieda lost several pilots in the last year. In the frantic effort to hold the enemy off who were getting closer to Germany, the risk to Ferry and Transport pilots had become much higher in the last year.

One day in the winter of 1944, Frieda got an urgent call to get a 109 fighter to the Russian Front but all her pilots were out on deliveries. She decided to do the delivery herself though she knew Al would be furious if he found out, but she decided to do it anyway. She picked up the 109 fighter at the factory. Just before takeoff, the tarmac superintendent insisted on arming the plane with ammunition and he told her that there was a good chance of meeting a Russian fighter. Everything went fine until she approached the front line airfield.

Suddenly, she spotted a MIG fighter diving at her in the little rear view mirror. She quickly did a slide slip with her flaps down, the MIG overshot her then Frieda gunned the throttle to full as the plane straightened out underneath the MIG. She came up under him in his blind spot and gave him a burst setting his fuel tank on fire. The Russian pilot rolled his plane over and bailed out. Frieda landed and taxied up following a lead vehicle to a designated place where a fighter pilot was waiting for his plane, and he immediately took off.

The Russian pilot had parachuted down to the edge of this temporary landing field and was captured. He was brought into the flight office for interrogation. When Frieda reported at the office the officer-in-charge mentioned to the Russian pilot that she was the pilot that shot him down. Frieda was amused at the stunned look on the Russian pilot's face; he was just a young lad about eighteen years old. Later on after they finished interrogating the young pilot, Frieda was talking to the commanding officer about what was going to happen to the young man. The officer told her that if the military police came here they would shoot him, but with the Russians being so close he didn't think the military police would want to be captured by the Russians, so they were staying closer to Germany. In the meantime, the pilot was put in a temporary cell.

While waiting to find out how she was going to get back to Berlin, she wandered over to the flight service area. While looking at one of the planes, she heard someone say aloud, "Frieda?"

She looked turned to see who said her name. It was Manfred Schultz, the head mechanic from the Berlin Flying Club, the one that had to repair the engines she burned out in the races she won. He was now a Sergeant in the Air Force. He realized his mistake at just calling her name and not addressing her rank. As he started to apologize, Frieda went over to him and gave him a friendly hug. She hardly recognized him, he must have been half starved, he was so thin and tired-looking, and tears came to his eyes as they talked. He told her she shouldn't be there; they were going to be attacked at any moment. He had been told to get the only JU52 ready to leave within a half hour. The officers were all getting out before the Russians captured and killed them.

Frieda asked Manfred what he was going to do. He told her he had an old JU50 single engine transport hidden in the woods under a camouflage cover. He managed to scrounge 400 liters of petrol and stored it in the JU50. She asked him if he had a pilot to fly it out, but with a sad look he said, "No, they are all leaving on the 52 in a few minutes. They already have a full plane. That's why they didn't invite you."

Frieda told Manfred to have the JU50 ready to go as soon as the others took off. She went into the office where the only officer left was busy gathering his things. She asked him what he was going to do about the young Russian pilot. He said, "I guess I'll have to shoot him."

She said, "Leave it to me; I'll take care of it." The officer, being relieved about not having to shoot the Russian and not bothering to ask Frieda if she wanted a lift back, dashed out to the waiting 52. As soon as he boarded the plane, it took off.

Frieda stood with Manfred and a bunch of mechanics watching the plane head towards Berlin. It had only gone about two kilometers when a Russian fighter attacked it. It was a sitting duck, being overloaded, flying slowly and not being able to do any maneuvering. The Russian pilot easily shot the plane before hitting the fuel tank. It burst into flames and exploded before hitting the ground. Frieda told Manfred to keep the 50 hidden until dark as it was too dangerous to try a getaway right now. She also went into the cell with Manfred to talk to the Russian youth. Manfred explained in broken Russian to the pilot who Frieda was and that she had just saved his life. He would be released just before they take off if he promised not to try to shoot her down again. Frieda put her hand out and a thankful youth with tears streaming down his face shook her hand.

As soon as it was dark, the JU50 was towed out of the hiding place in amongst the trees and one of the mechanics ran into the guard house and released the Russian. As they taxied toward the takeoff area, someone hollered, "He's waving to us." There in the dim light of the doorway to the office was the young pilot waving goodbye to them.

Manfred asked with a smile, "Do you know how to fly a 50?"

"Are you kidding? I cut my eye teeth on one of these when I was getting my Commercial Ticket. Even though this old bucket is overloaded with too many in it, it will lift off. It was designed to carry very heavy loads and be able to take off from mud or snow."

She had to use the landing lights to see the runway in the dark. Giving it full throttle, the 50 gradually gained speed. She remembered the take off speed was 95 km, but that was in an empty student plane; this one was overloaded, she was going to have to feel its correct speed to become airborne. The 50 with its big oversize wheels bounced along over the rough ground and when it hit 100 km, she could feel it gradually take flight and its airspeed slowly increase until it reached a safe speed to climb to 100 meters. The big BMW radial engine had its exhaust on the starboard side so she headed south for a few minutes, to keep the exhaust flame hidden from sight in case there were MIG fighters patrolling on the eastern side. Then, remembering the heading she used to get here from Berlin, she retraced her way back to Berlin with a thankful load of personnel.

As they approached Berlin they could see it was being bombed. No use trying to land there, either they would be shot down by friendly fire or get hit with a bomb, so she decided to head for the Club Field, but using the landing light there might expose that location to danger. Then she remembered the farm they had bought; it had a large unused pasture that could handle this overloaded slow landing transport. As she did a slow low circle of the field, a car came onto it and shone its headlights in the direction to land. There wasn't much light but enough to show the direction and where. Frieda held off with the landing lights and turned them on just in time to see the field and do a touchdown. She taxied back to the car to meet her guiding light even though she had a good idea who it was. When the engine stopped everybody leaped out of the plane. They all ran up to the person holding the flashlight. Just as Frieda figured, it was Al.

He said, "Where in the hell have you been? I've gone nuts trying to find you. When the bombing started earlier today I thought you might head here for safety. What happened and who are all these people?"

"Oh, I decided to go shopping and this is what I ended up with."

There was a big burst of laughter and Al said, "OK everybody into the house. I want to see who and what you brought and why."

When they all went into the house Al recognized several of the mechanics, and seeing how undernourished they were, he told them to be seated. He would get food for them. As the men ate, they eagerly told the whole story from where Frieda shot down the Russian MIG up to the landing here safely in Berlin.

Al had the feeling he was having a wild dream. He asked Manfred if he would go with him to make his report to the Fuhrer, which he agreed to do.

For safety reasons, Hitler has moved his head quarters into a bomb proof bunker and this was where Al took Manfred along with a written statement signed by Manfred. Of course they left out the part about what happen to the Russian pilot--they just stated he died in the crash of his plane. Besides, why kill the young man when the war was nearly over?

Hitler summoned Frieda to receive a medal for her bravery and he made sure a story about her heroism was published in the newspapers. While presenting the medal he told Frieda not to take any more chances, she was too important to Germany. After the ceremony he asked about the location of the JU50. Frieda said it was left on a farmer's field away from the airport and the Club Flying Field. Hitler showed a relieved smile and said, "Good. By the way, I understand you were once a nurse and I think it would be good publicity if you do some emergency nursing. See about getting a uniform so we can take some photos for the press and maybe also do some ambulance driving."

After Hitler left, Frieda said, "Hitler has a good feeling about where the JU50 is parked. Does that have anything to do with that Condor stored at the Club?"

"It sure has. He's got some scheme about bombing New York with it," Al admitted.

"What was that all about me wearing a nurse outfit and driving an ambulance? I don't know how to drive an ambulance!"

"What a crazy world. Here you are, a world famous aviatrix, flying transports and even fighter planes, shooting down an enemy fighter and you can't drive an automobile."

Al continued, "I have a feeling we'd better pull some strings and get you checked out on an ambulance very soon. I can't tell you why right now, but please be patient and go along with it all for both of our safe futures. Besides, you should know how to drive an automobile--you'll probably appreciate it later on. Please don't discuss anything we talk about with anyone. We are being watched and checked on by the Gestapo. They're going to look for a scapegoat to blame things on when this is all over, in order to cover their own tracks."

Within a week Frieda was signed on as a nurse-ambulance driver and Al taught her how to drive an auto. Just like her original handling of a plane, learning how to drive was easy and natural for her.

A general that was in charge of the concentration camps received a head injury during one of the bomb raids on Berlin. Hitler had invited the general and his wife to be his guests in the safe bunker. The next day, after having the general and his wife visit him and Eva in the bunker, he called Al in to discuss some of the air transportation problems he said they were having. Al figured it was an excuse to discuss something else and he wasn't surprised to hear the radio playing when he went in to see Hitler. He sensed this was going to be the answer to what Hitler had been scheming.

The first thing Hitler did was to order Al to turn his sidearm over to him. This made Al feel very uneasy but he was so curious to find out what was going to happen, he obliged.

With the radio playing and Hitler talking in low tones, he unveiled the plan he had been working on for all these years. To Al it sounded as though it was some kind of wild movie. As Hitler explained it, Al could see very clearly how he fitted into the plan. His original hunch was correct. It was an escape plan that had to have both Al and Frieda involved.

"Now I can see why you asked for my gun. I don't blame you, I'd do the same."

"Did you ever guess what the plan was?"

"Well, to be honest, I had a strong feeling and I tested you on several occasions because the puzzle was fitting close to what I felt. Now I know what part Frieda and I are to play. How do you plan to do the final cover-up?"

"That is the part that only Eva and I know about and it is best if you two don't know how it is done until we all are well out of Europe and in South America."

When the Russians were about three days away from taking Berlin, Hitler would order an ambulance to pick up a wounded person at the bunker. Frieda was to be the driver nurse; she will take the wounded man and his wife to the Flying Club where the Condor was waiting to take off. It was to be flown at night to Madrid where it will be fuelled up and proceed to Rinsque, then to South America and freedom.

The air raids on Berlin were hitting every other night. Hitler chose a night when there wasn't a raid. Al was at the emergency ambulance office expecting the call and when Frieda drove off, he headed for the Flying Club Field. He unlocked the huge hangar doors and pushed them open; the guard that was on duty gave him a hand to open the heavy doors, then Al told the guard to take the rest of the night off. He said the plane was going on a special mission and won't be back until the next day. Al used the small ramp tractor to tow the plane out to the runway. When he estimated that Frieda was nearing the field he started the engines.

The ambulance pulled up a few minutes later than Al figured. He helped a bandaged man and a woman into the plane, got them seated and buckled up, then a smiling Frieda joined him in the cockpit.

They estimated right. Having the Red Cross painted on the sides did the trick and they flew right to Madrid without any trouble. A few times they were checked out by Allied fighter planes but when the pilots saw this well lit plane displaying the Red Cross they evidently radioed to their bases that it was just a Red Cross plane and veered off after buzzing past it.

When they were about half way to Madrid, Hitler presented Al and Frieda with passports showing them as Swiss citizens along with their pictures and new names, Adam and Heidi Gross. They didn't bother going through Customs at Madrid; they just bought petrol with Swiss francs which Hitler provided, and they took off as soon as they finished the pre-flight checklist.

Al plotted a course direct to Rinsque. He planned to use the Lufthansa facilities there rather than the base at Dakar, which would probably be swarming with Allied personnel. It was a 2,800 kilometer flight and they would be over nine hours in the air. Al and Frieda had to spell each other off, so that on the leg from Berlin to Madrid they each managed to catch a couple of hours sleep. They were both tired even though they were exhilarated by the excitement of escaping to a new life and leaving a horrible war behind them. They would have to try to get some sleep on this leg of the flight to Rinsque. Al took the first four hour watch, but before doing so he asked both Eva and Adolph if they would come up to the cockpit once in awhile to see if the acting pilot is awake and also carry on a conversation with whoever is on duty.

During the first shift before Heidi tried going to sleep, she took Eva back to the plane's galley and showed her how to make breakfast for everyone. (Adam and Heidi had agreed that for their protection from now on they would call each other by their new names, Adam and Heidi Gross.)

On the last leg to Rinsque, Adam suggested Heidi ask Adolph to come up to the cockpit while she and Eva have some female talk. There were some things Adam wanted to talk to Adolph about before they got to Rinsque. Rather than get tangled up in the cramped co-pilot's seat, Adolph used the check pilot's seat right behind the captain's, which was more comfortable for him.

"I'm going to need funds to pay for the fuel at the next fuelling stations and also I'll need money when we get to Argentina for Heidi and I to live on. What provisions have you made?" Adam wasn't letting on that he already had a Swiss bank account, which by now contained enough to make him and Heidi reasonably well off.

"I have in my briefcase enough money to pay for all the fuel we will be using. As for your end of this venture I have opened an account in Switzerland under your name, Adam Gross, for five million francs, which should be enough to hold you over until you get established in Argentina," Adolph replied. "Here, I have written your Swiss account number on this note explaining all the necessary details for you. As for this plane, I'll leave that matter up to you as to how to dispose of it.

I'm very pleased you arranged to get the Condors. For some time I was concerned we would have to make this flight in one of the Heinkels. I shudder to think about it. By the way, call me Henry and Eva Marie. That is not the names on our passports but to protect all of us neither of you will ever know what names are on our passports, and please for your own safety, don't try to find out."

While Adam and Henry were involved in their discussion up in the cockpit, Heidi and Marie were busy in the galley preparing for an afternoon celebration. Heidi had picked up some supplies and champagne in Madrid from the airport caterer. Heidi set up some portable tables on the flight deck, and using the navigator, flight engineer, check pilot and the pilot seat they managed to have a celebration fiesta, and they toasted with champagne the start of a new life for all four of them.

Henry did a good job of disguising himself. He now had red hair, no moustache and wore glasses. He was just an ordinary person. Marie just looked plain, nothing outstanding, and they both emerged from their former selves like the phoenix.

They landed in Rinsque just before noon. On the flight down Adam wrote a note to be given to Em explaining that they were now Adam and Heidi Gross out of Switzerland and that he will contact Em later on from Argentina advising him of his address there. As soon as the plane landed he gave the service crew instruction to fill the plane with petrol. He was pleased to see it was a different crew from the one he dealt with originally. None of them knew him, not even the manager who was handling the sale. While the plane was being serviced, he phoned Em and asked him to come alone to the airport so they could have a meeting in his auto.

Adam didn't want to spend too much time on the ground. The war was still going on and even though it was expected that it would be over in a few days because the Russians were on the east side of Berlin and the Allies were on the west side, there was still a good chance there were spies at work, reporting events like a strange, big, Red Cross plane landing in Rinsque.

As soon as Em arrived at the airport Adam and Heidi got into the back of the limousine. Heidi gave Em a big hug and kiss while Adam and he shook hands. Adam handed Em the envelope with his instructions in it and Em gave Adam a big binder with all the details of their operation for the last seven years. Luckily, the limousine had dark glass at the rear seats so no one saw the transfer of information. Adam promised to bring Em up to date some day in the near future. Em noticed somebody looking out of the plane window at the car and he inquired as to who the passenger was. Adam explained it was a rich Jewish couple escaping from Europe. They said quick goodbyes with tears in their eyes. Adam then signed the sales slip for the fuel. He nearly signed Albert Wirth, but caught himself at the "A" and signed Adam Gross instead and paid with cash. He immediately got into the plane and with Heidi in the captain's seat the plane they took off from Rinsque and headed for the New World and an exciting start to a new life.

Chapter 9

ON THE FLIGHT across the South Atlantic Adam and
Heidi had quite a few discussions about the last few years and
what would be in store for them. For the first time since they were
married, it was possible to discuss openly what had happened.
Adam was always afraid to divulge too much to Heidi for her
own protection. The flight to South America was going to take
10 hours. They took advantage of this time alone on the flight
deck to discuss many things about the last ten years. He started
his story at the first meeting with Hitler at the banquet dinner
for Lufthansa.

"You had an idea of what was happening right from the
beginning, didn't you?" Frieda inquired.

"At first, I thought it was just by coincidence that my thoughts
and what he was talking about started to have a connection. He
has told me that at first he didn't have a plan. It was just an idea
or feeling that he had better start making a backup plan. It struck
him while he was talking to me at that first dinner, that I was the
key to a plan he could use because of my long-range flights and

experience. He didn't have his plan fully thought out until 1937. It was in that year he realized he had gone too far and couldn't back out--too far out on a dangerous limb."

"When did you realize that you were part of his plan?"

"At first I just considered it a jigsaw puzzle. I would place the things that were happening into the puzzle and gradually, by 1938, I had a pretty good idea of the picture. I would purposely suggest things to do with Lufthansa to see if they fitted into his plan, such as obtaining the Condors and the test flight to Argentina, which is when I really knew that both of us were part of his plan. Evidently, you were a key player in the final episode of the escape. Did you notice anything strange when you picked them up?"

"Yes, come to think about it. There were two things that I noticed: one was there was no guard on duty at the entrance to the Bunker and the other was a strong odor of kerosene when they got into the ambulance. At the time I didn't think too much about it because of the smells from the air raids. Do you think it could have something to do with his plan?"

"Yes I do, and we had better keep everything we have discussed to ourselves. I don't think we are completely out of the woods yet, so we had better watch our backs, keep close to each other and be very careful. It would be convenient if we both were killed in an accident; they would be home-free and no witnesses left to expose them. I'm going to have to create an insurance plan to protect us. As soon as I've hatched one I'll let you know. In the mean time they need us to get to Argentina."

Later, Heidi and Marie prepared sandwiches and coffee in the galley. They had taken off at one PM and, depending on the wind direction, they should arrive about ten PM, allowing for the time difference, so it was necessary to have at least two meals in flight. Henry and Marie used the handy little tables at their seats. Heidi and Adam ate at their seats on the flight deck and each took turns for a short nap and rest. Their interesting conversation made the time go faster and kept them from getting drowsy.

Adam had decided to land at Recife, like they did before, for two reasons: one, he was familiar with the landing approach; and two, Natal was an allied jumping off point to Africa. Even though the war has moved up into Europe and out of Africa, there could still be too many questions asked in Natal about this strange Red Cross plane and what it was doing here. There should be no trouble in Recife, Rio and Buenos Aires about the plane - he hoped. It was 9:45 PM when they circled the Recife Pan Am Airport and a field attendant switched on the landing strip lights as they touched down on the gravel runway. Adam noticed that there were two DC3s with Pan Am logos on them parked at the tarmac. Using Spanish, which the attendant understood, he requested the plane be refueled and ready for an eight AM take off the next morning. He then asked if they had to go through Customs if they stayed in the Pan Am Hostel. The attendant said they would not if they stayed in the hostel. Adam registered them all as the Grosses and requested to have breakfast at seven AM. He paid cash for everything in the morning and there was no trouble. They took off at eight AM.

It was on the leg from Recife to Rio that Adam and Henry had another discussion alone up in the flight deck.

"I'd like you to know that I have arranged for safety insurance for Heidi and me."

"What do you mean?"

"Well, to insure that nothing unexpected happens to us I have left a sealed envelope for a relative, containing everything about the escape. Of course, I had to second guess you on some of the details but I was positive about the escape flight to Argentina. It doesn't matter that they don't know what names we are using because I have arranged for the person to receive a monthly stipend as long as I'm alive or the seal on the envelope is not broken."

"You shouldn't have done that."

"Then you had better make sure nothing happens to Heidi or me."

Henry left the flight deck with a very concerned look on his face; Heidi noticed it when he came back into the cabin, so she immediately went up to Adam to find out what had happened. Adam told her what he had told Henry. She asked if it was true he had made such arrangements and he said yes, for her safety. Only he should know if it was true or not.

"How did you figure out such a scheme?"

"After ten years of playing the guessing game with him, I reasoned what he had to do to cover his tracks. The best way was to get rid of the only people who knew what had happened. There is a part of the puzzle I haven't figured out yet and that is what did he do down in the bunker to cover his tracks? I think we may find out something about that from the news when the war is over, or for some reason if he divulges that part to me."

"Well, you sure must have hit a nerve or you threw a monkey wrench into a plan he had because he sure was upset. He was swearing and carrying on like a mad man."

"By the way, have you found out what last name they have on their passports?"

"No, he refused to let me know earlier on. I figured that is another reason why I should advise him about the insurance plan I've arranged for to insure our safety. Keep your ears open when we go through Brazilian or Argentine Immigration. They may announce their names."

When they arrived at Rio they had to go through Customs and Immigration in order to stay at a hotel for the night, even though they all rode in the same taxi from the airport. Henry and Marie decided to go to a different hotel as they didn't think it was wise to all stay in the same hotel, and they agreed to meet Adam and Heidi at the airport before eight AM in the morning.

Both Heidi and Adam showered and went to bed as soon as they could. It had been an exhausting and trying trip even though they had done it just a few years previously.

The next morning Adam paid for the servicing and fuel in cash, signed the bill, and they took off just after eight in the morning. The flight to Buenos Aires was about 2,500 km, and it usually took 7 to 8 hours depending on the wind.

"How did they appear to you this morning?" Albert asked curiously.

"Marie spoke to me but I could feel the tension; she was definitely cool towards me," Heidi explained.

"Yes, I noticed it with Henry. I didn't expect for us to be social friends with them when we got to Buenos Aires but something is up between them. By the way I picked up a newspaper at the hotel just as we left, to see if there was any news in it about the war."

Heidi let out a kind of gasp, "You haven't read this yet?"

"No, what's up?"

"According to the headlines they found the burned remains of Hitler and Eva down in the bunker."

"I'm not surprised, Heidi. That smell of kerosene you mentioned earlier must have something to do with it; I wonder who the two souls they used were?"

"Have we any liquor on board?"

"Yes, when I was picking up provisions from the airport supplier I got a bottle of Scotch whisky because I haven't seen Scotch for several years let alone sipped it. Why?"

"Well as the old saying goes – candy is dandy, but liquor is quicker. I'm going to loosen his tongue with that Scotch. I hope it's not a waste of a good bottle. Just before we get to the border of Argentina I'm going to open that bottle and we are going to celebrate arriving in Argentina. I'll remain sober and try to find out what happened in the bunker. You had better stay sober too; we have to get through Customs and Immigration and also try to land this plane safely."

At 2:30 PM Adam marched out of the galley with the Scotch, four glasses and announced: "Happy hour time. We are now in Argentina." He poured hefty drinks of straight Scotch and said, "Here is to Buenos Aires." He took his and Heidi's glass up to the flight deck, making sure to leave the bottle with Henry and Marie. Heidi came back to the passenger cabin holding her glass and pretending to drink with them, then she left saying she was going to let Adam do some celebrating while she spelled him off. He had poured most of his drink down the washroom sink, then he refilled the glasses. It seemed to be working--both Marie and Henry were getting a little chatty. At the right moment Adam showed the newspaper to Henry and said, "That was brilliant. How did you do it?"

"Oh, that was just the General I had put in charge of the Concentration Camps. He was a sadistic slob and his wife was the meanest, cruelest person I had ever met. They were doomed to be shot by the Russians in a few days so I gave them the easy way out, poisoned them both. After I sent the guards home to their families, I poured kerosene over everything and set it all on fire, did the world a favor."

Then, when Adam went back to relieve Heidi at the controls, she anxiously asked, "Get anything?"

"Yes, I got the whole story. You'd better go back and try to sober them up before we land. I'll tell you the whole thing when we get in our hotel room tonight; it's pretty much like what I figured happened. Let's get this thing down and start our new life."

Before they left the plane, Adam told Henry to give him two thousand francs. He needed cash for living expenses and to set up a small bank account. Henry didn't want to co-operate until Adam pulled his hand gun out from under his coat and said, "Now it's three thousand or you don't get off the plane – in one piece."

A reluctant Henry put his brief case on his lap and cautiously lifted the lid to conceal the contents. He pulled out a wad of bills and counted out three thousand Swiss Francs and begrudgingly handed them to Adam. Marie was staring at Adam; if looks could kill he'd be dead.

Henry said, "What are you going to do with the plane?"

"We should just walk away from it like it was an airliner we had just come in on. It's the one thing that can link us to Germany. Just abandon it; they will eventually seize it for airport taxes. If Lufthansa is restarted after the war, let them argue it out with the Argentine authorities about the ownership.

Adam saw a map of Argentina on the seat along side of Henry. He noticed a circle around a location on the map and made a mental note of it. Henry saw Adam looking at the map and he casually folded it up.

Adam asked, "Where will you head for? There are pockets of Germans throughout Argentina; I'm going to avoid them and I think it would be wise for you to do so also."

"We haven't decided yet, it'll probably be on the coast somewhere. What about you?"

"Oh, I think we will get lost in the crowd of Buenos Aires somewhere. By the way, Heidi and I will depart the plane first. Wait at least fifteen minutes for us to clear Immigration, then you both depart. Otherwise we will all end up in detention if you don't do as I say. I have gone through these procedures hundreds of times and I know the routine."

By the time Adam and Heidi gathered what little luggage they had brought and opened the exit door, the airport ramp workers had rolled the portable stairs up to the plane's door. Adam and Heidi casually walked up to the Customs and Immigration entrance, the Custom's officer did a brief inspection of their luggage and motioned for them to proceed to the Immigration Officer. Adam and Heidi both presented their Swiss passports to the Officer. After looking at the passports and at them, he asked in French, what was the nature of their visit to Argentina? Adam replied in French that it was a business trip. The official smiled and said in French, "Welcome to Argentina."

Both Adam and Heidi smilingly breathed a sigh of relief and headed out the airport door into Argentina and got into a taxi. In Spanish, Adam told the driver to take them to the nearest hotel. Luckily it was not the same hotel they used on their first trip to Argentina, as they didn't want to be recognized by any of the staff.

After having a much-needed shower, they went to the hotel dining room and had a late but very enjoyable dinner, drinking the delicious Argentine wine with their roast beef entrée.

That night in bed, Adam told the story of Hitler's escape to a horrified Heidi. She asked what happened in the plane with him and Henry, just before they departed. He explained how he forced Henry to give him an extra thousand francs and how he possibly saw where Henry and Marie are headed to. He also suggested they had to refrain from using Henry's previous name for their own security.

"Have you considered where we should head for?"

"Yes, I started to gather information about Argentina several years ago. I talked to pilots that have flown here and studied the maps of Argentina. A place I think would be nice to live in is Bahia Blanca. It's about 300 km down the coast from Buenos Aires. We should go down there and size it up before making any definite decision. Tomorrow morning we have to go to a bank and do some transferring of funds."

Adam explained to Heidi about the 500,000 franc gift from Henry. It should be transferred into an Argentine bank before it gets traced or before Uncle Henry decided to steal it back because he had the account number.

Chapter 10

"I HAVE ANOTHER Swiss account I couldn't tell you about, it's one that Em set up. We have shares in a business with Karl Andersen. It is a private company that supplies the fuel for airplanes and ships in West Africa. Here's the binder Em gave me at the Rinsque airport. Let's have a look now--I haven't had a chance to look at it since he gave it to me."

He handed the profit and loss sheet to Heidi without looking at it first.

She exclaimed, "My God, if this is true you are a very rich man! Did you have any Idea of how much you have in that Swiss Account?"

"No, the last sheet I saw was in 1938 when we did that test run down here. How much is there?"

"Well, according to this statement, there are two million in US dollars and three million in Swiss Francs. But why?"

"The war: we supplied all sides with fuel and they were glad to get it. Being a private company supplying all sides we couldn't display any company signs during the war, that's why there is no letterhead on the company report. For security reasons and our safety the name of the company has to be kept secret. Remember that first trip when you asked me what I was smiling about after that first meeting with Em. Well this was the premonition I had, doing business with Swiss bank accounts and becoming rich."

"OK, you rich, lucky son of a bitch, I want to make love to a millionaire in Argentina. Let's go to bed."

The next day both Adam and Heidi went into the Banque de Argentina to see the manager and arrange the transfer of the 500,000 francs. Luckily they had the extra cash from Henry, because it took seven days to clear the bank transfer. They spent their time taking tour trips and especially one down the coast to Bahia Blanca, which turned out to be a resort area with nice haciendas on the waterfront for rich Argentines. Later on, they flew down on a charter plane, stayed at a resort hotel, rented an auto and drove around looking at the villas that were for sale. Finally they went to a real estate broker in the town of Bahia Blanca who specialized in waterfront country estates. He eventually showed them one of the waterfront haciendas they had looked at but hadn't known it was for sale. After showing them the entire estate complete with swimming pool, dock for launch and a beautiful home, they finally agreed on a price which was less than expected. Because of the war, prices of the properties were depressed, even here in Argentina. It was even fully furnished; all they had to do was replenish the food supply.

After living in this lovely hacienda for about a month, a gardener-caretaker came to see them. He explained that he was the original gardener and his wife was the housekeeper-cook for this place before the owner went broke because of the war. The owner was a cattle baron and when Europe went to war he couldn't ship any more beef, so he had to liquidate to save from losing everything he owned. This was the first place he turned over to the bank after going broke. Adam and Heidi liked the gardener and his wife so they were hired as live-in employees, making life much easier for the Grosses.

There is a house at the gated entrance that was originally used by the servants. Jose and his wife Eva requested to move into it and live there again, which the Grosses gladly agreed to.

It wasn't long after they had moved into their hacienda, the radio announced the war was over in Europe and the war criminals were going to be tried in Nuremberg. Evidently Adolph Hitler had escaped the trial by committing suicide with his companion Eva Braun in the Berlin bunker. There was no mention of a missing Focke Wulf Condor transport. Apparently, on one of the bombing raids everything at the Flying Club had been destroyed, according to one of the reporters covering the news from Europe.

The housekeeper, Eva, and Heidi got along very well, even though Heidi couldn't speak Spanish, but with Eva's help it was only a matter of a few months before Heidi came to understand Spanish better each day. It was essential if they were going to live in Argentina for the balance of their lives.

On June 12, 1946, Heidi gave birth to a boy, Albert Gross. This was the icing on their cake, making their life in Argentina complete, despite their age, as Adam was 46 and Heidi 39.

In September of 1947 there was a news report about a Swiss man and his wife burned beyond recognition in an auto accident in the mountain region of Mendosa, Argentina. Adam looked up the location on a map and realized that it was the location he saw on Henry's map.

When he talked it over with Heidi she remarked, "Do you think those devils pulled the same stunt again to do some more track covering?"

"I don't know, but it sure is a coincidence. Maybe they did something to expose themselves and were murdered. I know the Jewish underground is catching escaped Nazis and I wouldn't put it past them to hold a quick tribunal of their own rather than let some high priced lawyer argue their case and let them go on living as a slap in the face to all those who suffered from concentration camps."

"Do you think we might be on a wanted list?"

"No, but we had better be careful. We were involved in the great escape. If Henry and Marie were tortured to get information we could be targeted. You'd better dye your hair to a different colour, maybe blonde, and change the style to longer; you'd look even sexier and different. Remember, you were well known as the famous woman aviatrix."

One day in September 1948 Jose, Eva's husband, called Adam aside while working out in the rose garden. Pretending they were talking about the flowers, Jose explained that two strange men had been asking a lot of questions around the district about the Grosses. Most of the neighbors refused to talk to them and some who did gave only vague information. The men showed a photograph of a Frieda Schmidt taken from a newspaper story about her winning the Berlin/Marseille race. Adam felt his blood turn cold when Jose told him about the two men. He asked Jose if he had talked to the men and Jose said he had briefly, when they showed him the photo. Adam asked if Jose could detect a dialect from their speech, and Jose said he thought it was Russian. Adam thought maybe they were Russian Jews. He felt sick; they must be on to Heidi and him if they were this close. He immediately went into the hacienda and told Heidi the whole story. She broke down and cried, saying that she thought it was all too good to be true-- this wonderful life they were having.

"What should we do?"

"We'll have to be very careful, stay in the house and be very careful. The most they could do is to kidnap us and take us back to Germany for a trial; I don't think we are on a war crimes list."

The very next day two men appeared at the door and the younger man asked, "Is Frieda Wirth home?"

Adam was about to say "no, she isn't," but the way the man spoke in a friendly voice prompted Adam to reply, "Who should I say is calling?"

"My name is Tomaso Sklarenko. I doubt if she would recognize it, we met briefly several years ago. I think we should have a talk. I have some important information for both of you."

"Will you please wait at the door. I'll get her."

Adam found Heidi in the den, crying, Adam put his arms around her and told her that he didn't think they were in trouble. This man had something important he wanted to talk about.

When Heidi went to the door the younger man smiled at her and said, "You never knew my name, but I knew yours. You saved my life in 1945." He was smiling and Heidi could see he had tears in his eyes as he spoke. She said, "Would you please come in? I'd like to hear your story."

She led both men into the den and asked them to take a seat; both Adam and Heidi were bewildered and anxious to hear what this man had to say.

"As I told Albert, my name is Tomaso Sklarenko and this gentleman is Nicolas Panamaroff. He is an agent for the Russian Federal Police. We both did investigation of war criminals for the Nuremberg Trial--he as a policeman and I as a reporter. We found it convenient to collaborate on our findings. Especially on the strange disappearance of the Focke Wulf Condor that was stored at the Berlin Flying Club hangar. We could not find any evidence that it had been destroyed in a bombing raid; there was no debris that should have been there if the plane had been destroyed in the raid. The plane had vanished. Also the person I was seeking to thank for saving my life had vanished along with her husband, Albert Wirth. Are you getting the picture yet, Colonel Wirth?"

"Are you the young pilot I shot down?"

"Yes, and we are here to tell you how we returned the favour for saving my life. At the preliminary investigation that put names on the war crimes list, because of your ranks, both your names were on it. Nick here, knowing you had saved my life, asked me to appear at the preliminary meeting to appeal your cases. We stated that neither of you had been involved in any human crime and when Nick asked me to present my testimony about you saving my life, and seeing there was no other evidence against either of you, your names were struck off the list. You both are home free. You can both go back to Germany and not worry about being hunted."

Both Frieda and Al sat there with tears in their eyes.

Al poured a glass of sherry for everyone to toast the occasion.

Then he inquired, "How in the hell did you find us?"

Tomaso laughed. "It sure wasn't easy. We nearly gave up several times. It was the Condor, we traced it to Argentina, and then, using government pull and payoffs, we followed the paper trail, the large deposits from Switzerland and finally the transfers to the local branch here in Bahia Blanca. If you hadn't been a famous woman pilot, I doubt we would have found you; it was your press photos that did it."

Al invited them to stay the night with them, but they both said they had better get going because they had to get the rental car back and would just make it in time to catch their return flight on the Lufthansa Condor. They said it was strange that this Condor was the only one in the Lufhansa fleet that was painted white.

That night the couple went to bed as Al and Frieda Wirth. For the first time in three years they could be their true selves and not live with the weight of a lie over them.

They had quite a discussion about theirs and young Albert's future. They realized that it was known how they escaped, by using the Condor, but they could never divulge what they know about Hitler and Eva or they could be tried for assisting a war criminal. They decided that they should keep the name Gross and remain in Argentina and carry on with their new life. After all, they are well off living at a beautiful place in a big hacienda with servant's help who have two children for young Albert to play with. Why go back to Germany with all those bad memories of the war? Why expose young Albert to it?

In 1949 they bought a Mercedes sedan, which Frieda, Al and Jose drove to go shopping and touring around the country. Jose used it to take his children to school, and in 1952 when little Albert started school, he rode with the other children in the car to the school in Bahia Blanca It was if they were all one family. Albert spent the first six years of his life growing up and playing with the Font children. He spoke Spanish like a native; all the other children at school believed that Albert and the other children were all related. With his dark hair like his mother's, he was considered to be an Argentine Spaniard.

Chapter 11

MANY TIMES JOSE felt as though he were being watched when driving the children. He couldn't explain it, so he didn't mention it to Adam. Then, one day, he realized that a Mercedes sedan like the one he was driving, only with black glass windows on its sides, was parking near the school when Jose was picking up the children. At first he thought the car was there to pick up a child, but one day he purposely waited and watched the car. It didn't pick anyone up and finally it drove off. Jose reported what he had seen to Adam, so the next day Adam rode with Jose when he was taking the children to and from school. He did this several times but no automobile was seen fitting the description that Jose described. Adam carried his automatic handgun as a precaution and for protection. After several days of trying to identify if there was someone in a Mercedes observing them, they dismissed it as just a coincidence, but Adam told Jose to keep a sharp lookout and watch the children, making sure they were safe.

One day as Jose was waiting for the youngsters, he arrived at the school on time but Albert didn't come out. When Jose went into the school he was told by the teacher that Albert's aunt and uncle had already picked him up to take him to the hospital where his parents were. They told the teacher that Albert's parents had been injured in an accident and were at the hospital. The child was rushed out before the teacher could check their story.

Jose was fit to be tied; he rushed home as fast as he could drive and told two terrified parents the awful news. They immediately phoned the police; by the time the police got to their hacienda the kidnappers were long gone. Jose did his best to help the police with any information he could give. The police talked to the teacher and got the description of the kidnappers. The description threw Adam and Heidi off their original suspicion, they had immediately thought about Hitler and Eva, but the ones described were younger. So they concluded that it was for ransom money that Albert was kidnapped. The police said they should expect a phone call or letter demanding a ransom very soon.

That very night Adam took a phone call from which a voice told him to get that insurance letter, they would give him the instructions as to where to send it at a later date.

Adam and Heidi now both knew whom they were dealing with. Heidi's first suspicion about that report of two Swiss people being killed in an auto fire had been confirmed. They couldn't use the police. Somehow, they had to get Albert back by their own means. But how could they do it?

That night Adam and Heidi had a long discussion about what to do. Who could they call on for help and what could be done? They decided they had to call on someone they could trust to help them. How could they get help without divulging who the kidnappers really were?

They decided to reveal that the two people they brought out from Germany were a General who was in charge of the Concentration Camps and his wife. They had kidnapped Frieda at gunpoint after hearing that the Condor was stored at the Flying Club. They first contacted Al and offered him 500,000 Swiss francs that would be placed in a Swiss account; the account number would be given to Al when they reached Argentina, if he would fly them there. He refused to have anything to do with them. That's when they kidnapped Frieda and forced Al to fly them out of Germany to Argentina. They had already arranged for their Swiss bogus passports. Al and Frieda had obtained theirs through the black market in the beginning of 1945 when it was obvious the Germans were going to lose the war.

Albert, being a General, assumed he would be tried along with the other Nazis for war crimes, even though he had no part in the atrocities. He decided a year before that he and Frieda would use the spare Condor to make their escape. Several of the top Nazis were making plans to escape at the last minute in planes. Rudolph Hess jumped the gun and flew himself to Scotland in a Messerschmitt 110 several months ahead of time, knowing they had lost the war. Several of the top brass had planes like the Fieseler Storch and Messerschmitt 108s ready to be used for escape, but in most cases, the pilots merely took off before the Russians got there saving their own skins from the Russian onslaught.

Adam and Heidi gathered most of their proposed story from information drawn from newspaper articles about the fall of the Nazi regime around Berlin. Also, a lot was gathered from their discussions with Tomaso Sklarenko and Nicholas Panamaroff when they were visiting Heidi and Adam.

They typed their story out like a manuscript using two copies so they both could study and perfect their scenario of what happened. When they were satisfied their story would hold up without revealing what really happened, they destroyed the copies. Then Adam phoned Em and told the story of what happened. Em wanted to come to them right away, but Adam asked Em to contact Tomaso Sklarenko at the Moscow newspaper and Nicholas Panamaroff via Tomaso. Adam would pay everyone's airfare and expenses if they would come out and help recover young Albert from his Nazi kidnappers.

When Adam phoned Em, he said, "Em, Heidi and I have a big problem. Our son, Albert, has been kidnapped and we need help to recover him. Heidi remembered what you said about writing and being interested in mystery stories and solving them. Also we could use the help of a Moscow reporter named Tomaso Sklarenko and his friend Nicholas Panamaroff who is with the Russian Federal Police. They were very helpful to us and are experts at tracking Nazi war criminals. We would appreciate it if you could contact Tomaso and persuade them both to hunt down the Nazi that has got our little Albert. Of course we will pay all their expenses. We would also like for you and Marie to come and stay with us. Heidi could use Marie's companionship right now."

Em asked Adam for Tomaso's address or phone number, which Adam gave to him from a card Tomaso had left him.

"Adam, I'm very sorry to hear about the kidnapping, I realize you both are going through a terrible period in your life. Just leave the arrangements up to me. As soon as I get the arrangements made with this Mr. Sklarenko I'll let you know, and Marie and I will be out on the next plane that we can get to Argentina. Hang in there and give our love to Heidi."

Em phoned back that same night and told Adam that he had wired the funds to Tomaso for his and Nicholas's expenses. He said, "I had no trouble convincing Tomaso, as soon as he found out that it involved a Nazi war criminal. He affirmed that he and Nicholas would be down to Argentina as soon as possible. They will probably be there in a day or two, about the same time Marie and I should arrive. You'd better stay close to the phone to receive any instructions they will give you."

"Thanks a million, Em. I'll send Jose to pick you up at the airport. Let me know what flight you'll be on and approximately your time of arrival. If Tomaso and Nicholas are on the same flight, Jose will bring them also. There is plenty of room here at our hacienda, Casa del Mar. There are lots of bedrooms--Tomaso and Nicholas can use this place as their headquarters while doing their search. Heidi and I sure appreciate the help you're giving us – thanks again, Em."

The next day after talking to Em, Adam received a phone call, telling him to send the letter in another sealed envelope to Senor A. Gonzales, Post Office Box 118, Buenos Aires Post Office. Adam stalled the caller whose voice he recognized as Hitler's by saying he had to have about a week to receive the letter from his relative. He then told Hitler he wanted to speak to his son to make sure he was safe and well. They argued about this request for a few moments before Hitler would let the boy say that he was all right over the phone to Adam.

When he hung up Heidi wanted to know what was said: "I wish you had never said that there was such a letter."

"Heidi, if I hadn't used the letter as an insurance to keep us alive we wouldn't have lived this long. They would have murdered us the first chance they got. Right now that letter is the thing that is keeping Albert alive. We have to have proof that Albert is alive and well or they don't get the letter and we are not giving them the letter until we get Albert back.

Thinking back about the description of the kidnapper the teacher gave, I believe it was Hitler and Eva made up to look younger in a disguise. I don't believe Hitler would trust anyone else in on this plot. It would be too foolish for him to do so; he is too clever to do that, it could blow his cover. When he spoke on the phone he used Spanish and tried to disguise his voice. At first it threw me off but now I am sure it was Hitler. From now on we will have to remember to stick to the scenario we decided on and only mention the name General Hans Kruger. We should keep rehearsing our story until we believe it ourselves and there will be no slip-ups. By the way, Em said he and Marie expect to be here in a few days. Tomaso and Nicholas might be arriving at the same time so we'd better get stocked up on our provisions."

For the next two days Heidi and Adam rehearsed the scenario they agreed on, knowing that the presentation and belief of their story has a direct connection to their future and the safe return of Albert.

On the third day after the kidnapping, Jose drove up to the Buenos Aires Airport. Luckily, they all came in on the same flight. Em didn't know Tomaso and Nicholas by sight so when he arrived at the airport he had them paged, just in case they were on the same flight. Luckily they were, so after introductions were exchanged, they all piled into the Mercedes driven by Jose, heading for the Hacienda Casa del Mar at Bahia Blanca,

On the trip from Buenos Aires, the passengers took advantage of the time spent in the car to question Jose about what happened and to discuss it amongst themselves.

Em, being interested in mystery novels, presented his view of the crime from a writer's perspective. Tomaso and Nicholas just kept asking questions and not divulging any of their thoughts. They had always worked as a team, each pulling a thread and going over it carefully together until they had located a trail to work on. They both thought alike and they knew how and where to look to find evidence leading to a trial.

Just to be sociable and break the monotony of the trip they had discussions with Marie and Em trying to find out what connection they had with the Wirths. Who were they, where do they come from and how did they meet the Wirths? Em was careful not to mention his business dealings with Al; he only mentioned that they knew Al and Frieda through their dealings with Lufthansa, and they had become good friends. Marie related how Adam and Heidi became engaged, then had their wedding at Em's Palace. In their discussions it became apparent that Em and Marie preferred to use the names Adam and Heidi. They suggested that maybe Tomaso and Nicholas do the same because that is now the proper names of the couple. The two men agreed and said they would take note of that and change their files to use the Gross names instead of Wirth.

In the discussion, Em mentioned that he did notice another person in the plane when it was getting fuelled up at Rinsque. He stated that Adam appeared a little concerned when asked who the persons in the plane were and that he explained it as a wealthy Jewish couple who were escaping out of Europe. Em said that, at the time, he didn't think too much about it but as he thought more about it later, he realized that if he were writing a novel about this story he wouldn't mention that the couple was Jewish. He would say instead that they were a German couple trying to get out of Europe, unless he was trying not to divulge who they were.

Both Tomaso and Nicholas became very interested in the information about the other people in the plane. Evidently they considered it vital to solving who had kidnapped young Albert.

They arrived at the hacienda Casa del Mar about 11:30 AM. Adam and Heidi were both at the door to greet them. First Marie and Em gave them hugs and kisses expressing their feelings about the situation, and then both Tomaso and Nicholas shook hands with the Grosses assuring them that they would do everything possible to get Albert back safe and sound. Both Adam and Heidi thanked them for coming and Jose and Eva took the luggage up to the guest bedrooms that had been designated. Heidi suggested everyone use the washrooms, then come down to the dining room for lunch. Eva had made a large pot of her favourite vegetable soup along with tasty luncheon buns.

Knowing that all the guests would be tired after the long flights, Adam and Heidi insisted they all have afternoon naps before dinner, then they could get down to working on the case after.

Both Adam and Heidi were thankful they had bought this mansion with so many rooms in it. They didn't think at the time of purchase that it would ever be needed for an occasion such as this. They were thankful that they had Casa del Mar but sad that it had to be used for such a tragic situation.

After she has rested Marie told Heidi that she wanted to help her and Eva with the dinner. The three women wanted to keep occupied. Jose was busy working in the yard and keeping an eye out for security reasons, and then he had to go to pick up his children from school. As the men come down from resting, Adam took them into the den where Jose had lit a fire in the fireplace. Adam poured them all a drink to help loosen things up and to help with the discussions they were having.

It was a shame that such a wonderful dinner was used for such a sad occasion. But Heidi assured herself that after they get Albert back, they were going to do this again someday. Both Tomaso and Nicholas had never seen such a large and delicious roast beef dinner because of the suffering Russia was still undergoing from the war.

Eva had to go to their quarters to feed her family and take care of things there. Heidi told her not to bother with the rest of the dinner, she and Marie would attend to the serving of dessert. Eva could do the clean up after she had finished at her place.

Heidi and Marie cleared everything off the big dinner table so it could be used as a conference table. Tomaso asked Adam if it would be all right if Nicholas chaired the meeting because this was his profession. He was an expert at compiling information for investigations. Adam was pleased that these two professionals were going to help get Albert back safe and sound.

Heidi asked if it was all right for her and Marie to stay out of the meeting; they wanted to go into the den where they could have a good chat with each other. The men all agreed that it'll be good for Heidi to have Marie to talk to and be consoled.

Nicholas took a pad and pen out of the briefcase he brought along, and then he said, "Al, I'm going to start at the beginning and the questions I am going to ask pertain only to this case. First, I understand there was someone else in the plane with you and Heidi when you brought it out from Germany. Can you tell us who it was?"

"Yes, it was General Hans Kruger and his wife."

Both Tomaso and Nicholas flashed surprised looks at each other. "Are you sure?"

"Well, I only met him once before and that was a week before we escaped. It was at the Bunker when Heidi was getting a medal from Hitler for saving several ground personnel from the Eastern Front."

"How come he and his wife ended up on the plane?"

"The night we left, Heidi (Frieda) was called to the bunker to pick up a wounded person. She was doing volunteer ambulance driving so I went along with her to give her a hand in case she needed help. When we got to the bunker, the General and his wife got into the ambulance and demanded to be taken on the Condor. I told him that it was being held for Hitler. The General showed me a draft for 500,000 Swiss francs and said it was mine if I would take them on the Condor. I asked about Hitler and Eva and he said that they won't be needing the Condor, they have made other plans. When I refused they grabbed Heidi and threatened to shoot her if we didn't get moving right away.

I thought that because I was a General I would be considered a war criminal by the Russians so I had no alternative but to get in the Condor and takeoff immediately with Heidi being held at gunpoint. When we landed at Rinsque they threatened to kill all of us if we didn't cooperate with them. That is why I couldn't divulge to Em who was in the plane. I didn't want to take a chance on a shoot up by those two psychos. When we landed at Madrid for refueling I managed to get a bottle of Scotch that I planned for Heidi and I to use for a celebration when we got safely to South America. When we were almost to Argentina I suggested to the General and his wife that we have a celebration for reaching freedom and South America, so I produced the bottle of Scotch. They gorged on the booze and both got drunk. I removed their weapons and the draft for the 500,000 Swiss francs. I searched their luggage for more weapons and found none. Heidi and I locked ourselves into the flight deck until we reached Buenos Aires. They must have hidden their passports somewhere on their bodies because we couldn't find the passports, so we never knew what name they were using.

While searching them, I robbed enough cash off them to carry us over until we got the draft into our account in Buenos Aires. We departed the plane before them and never saw them or heard from them until now. I knew they would hunt us down in trying to cover their tracks, so I concocted the story about a letter of insurance to protect us."

"Have you any idea where they headed for in Argentina?"

"Yes, one time I got a glance of a map they were using. It had an area circled. Later on when I got a map of Argentina, I checked it to see where the area was. I believe it is near a town called Mendoza in the province of Mendoza up in the foothills of the Andes."

Nicholas turned to Tomaso and asked, "What do you think?"

"It sounds like the Krugers. They are the cruelest and most blood thirsty of all the Nazis we have been looking for. They probably murdered Hitler and Eva so they could take their place in the plane. Adam, did you notice anything different about them when they got into the ambulance?"

"Yes Tomaso. Both Heidi and I noticed it but we didn't think anything about it until later when we were discussing what happened at the Bunker. It was the strong odor of kerosene. At first we thought it was one of the smells from the bombing, but it stayed in the ambulance as though it was on their clothes."

Tomaso turned to Adam and Em. "This Hans Kruger was the commandant at Auschwitz, the worst of the concentration camps. He must have found out how Hitler was going to escape and tortured them into telling him how they were going to do it, and then murdered them to take their places in the plane. Adam, you are lucky they didn't kill one of you and use the other to fly the plane, but I guess they realized they needed both of you to reach South America. Well Nicholas, I guess our search should start in the Mendoza region."

Adam told them that the kidnappers would recognize his Mercedes, so he would go into town and purchase a car for them to use.

Nicholas told Adam to buy an older car that runs well; they didn't want to be obvious.

The next day, right after breakfast, Adam and Jose went into Bahia Blanca and purchased a green1946 Mercedes diesel sedan and registered it in Jose's name. Tomaso and Nicholas had asked Jose to go along with them to do the driving and he could be helpful with the interpretation and questioning. Also if the police stopped them, the owner would be driving and could explain the situation and maybe gain some information from the police about the ones they were looking for.

Tomaso explained that Argentina was not cooperative in getting Nazis out of the country, but in this case they were looking for kidnappers of Argentine descent, so they would have to use that approach when questioning people.

Em said he wanted to go with them to help with the hunt, but Tomaso said that it would be better if just Jose went with them for now. Maybe later on they might come back to take Em and Marie with them to make it look like they were tourists.

Right after lunch the search party headed west out of Bahia Blanca. About fifty kilometers west, they came to the edge of the great pampas region covered In rolling plains of wheat and cattle. There was nowhere here the kidnappers could hide so they pressed on to the town of Mercedes. After they got settled in a hotel they started their search, asking in restaurants and hotels about two Europeans, a man and woman, that moved into the area about six or seven years ago. They drew a blank; no trace of the Krugers.

The next day they drove to the village of San Luis and checked it out, without results. Jose was becoming despondent, but Nicholas and Tomaso assured him they would find the kidnappers. It takes a lot of work and perseverance to track fugitives down. They had done it for years and one of the few to escape them was the Krugers.

The next day after the search party left, Adam took the phone call from the kidnapper who wanted to know whether they had received the letter yet. Adam told him that it was coming by special courier; he didn't trust the mail with such an important letter. He tried to quiz the caller about instructions on getting the letter to him, but the connection cut off.

Em and Marie were a great help in consoling the Grosses. Adam and Heidi were fretting because they hadn't heard anything from the searchers. Em told them at this point that no news is good news, because they were still searching and will give an update as soon as they get a lead on a trail. Both Adam and Heidi expressed their gratitude for Em and Marie being there to help during the stressful time they were having.

When the searchers reached the town of Mendoza, they had a pretty good idea of the questions to ask to receive a sympathetic response with people who were willing to help find the kidnappers of a child. While looking around they noticed a Mercedes Auto Dealership. The manager was reluctant to give any information until he was told it involved a kidnapping and the police were eventually going to be involved and would be asking a lot of questions and looking at records. The manager eventually let them go over the purchase records for the past six years. They found the sale of a Mercedes fitting the description Jose gave. The sales person who handled the sale vaguely remembered that the two Swiss people paid by cheque. The address was on the sales slip along with information about the bank that was used in Buenos Aires.

The address given was a place west of the town up near the Andes Mountains. They got a local map of the area and headed up there right away. They wanted to observe the place without causing any disturbance that could endanger young Albert's life. They drove by the place twice in the daytime and then after dark they parked the car and walked cautiously up the side of the estate, observing it through a high wire fence that had a cattle fence charge on it. It was not enough to kill but enough to bounce one off the fence if they touched it.

The house was like a Swiss chalet in design. By using their binoculars they could see there were very few lights on and the only sign of life was that of an elderly man who appeared to be a caretaker.

The next day they went to the town of Mendoza's City Hall to check the Land Registry records to see if they could get the name on the title. Jose explained to the clerk these were two Swiss businessmen who were interested in that property and they would like to find out who owned it so that they can have a look at it.

The clerk, without looking at the records, told them it belonged to the Mendels. Jose asked her how she knew that without looking at the records and she explained.

"That's easy. My grandfather is the caretaker there. The Mendels are away on a business trip at the moment."

Jose asked, "Do you think we could talk to your grandfather about the place this afternoon as my friends have to leave tomorrow on a business trip?"

She phoned to the chalet and spoke to her grandfather, stating that they just wanted to talk about the place and not go inside it. He agreed, they thanked her and headed out there immediately.

The caretaker met them at the gate after he tied up the two Doberman watchdogs.

They asked him all sorts of questions about the house and the occupants in a friendly manner. They found out that the Mendels had driven down south to San Rafael to look at another estate. He even got the address from a note pad on their desk and brought it out to them. They suggested to the grandfather not to mention anything to the Mendels because they might get mad at him for talking to strangers about their chalet.

The next day they drove to the address in San Rafael. It turned out to be just an ordinary house, nothing like the sort of house the Mendels would be buying. While they were watching the house a man came out and got into a car. They followed him to the village food market. Jose followed him into the market and approached him. When Jose asked the man if he knew the Mendels the man turned and ran out of the market to his car, but Tomaso and Nicholas were waiting at the car for him. They told him to get in the back of the car with one of them while the other two got in the front seat.

Jose asked, "Why did you run?"

"Who are you? What do you want with me?" the frightened man retorted.

Jose asked, "Do you know the Mendels?'

"Yes, I was their gardener but they let me go because I wouldn't do something for them."

Jose inquired, "What was it you refused to do?"

"They wanted me to pick up a child in Bahia Blanca. They said it was their child that had been abducted from them in Switzerland and they wanted him back."

"Why did you refuse?" Jose wondered.

"I didn't trust them. They were not nice people. I gave them the name of a cousin over in Realico. I think they went to see him."

"Do you see these two men? They are from the Secret Police. If you breathe a word of this you will go to jail for a long time. Comprende?" The man nodded, he understood and drove away in a hurry. Jose said they had better stay here at the inn in San Rafael for the night because there wasn't any lodging in Realico. It was all farming community around that area, and also they had better phone Adam and let him know what they had found out.

They phoned Adam and told him they had found out the name the kidnappers were using and that they were on their trail.

That same day the kidnapper phoned Adam and asked about the letter. Adam told him he wouldn't tell him anything more until he talked to Albert. He wanted to make sure he was alive and well before any further arrangements were made. Mendel became belligerent on the phone but Adam stuck by his demand. Mendel said he would put Albert on the phone tomorrow night.

Adam assumed that Mendel was using a pay phone; also, he heard the sound of a train that didn't appear to be traveling fast, like it was going through a rural town, maybe a freight train. Adam was making notes of anything he noticed or of what was said.

The three hunters left San Rafael early in the morning heading east back towards Bahia Blanca. Realico was in the Pampas region and they arrived there just before lunchtime. The cousin they were looking for was Renaldo Font and he worked in the office of a grain company in Realico. They waited outside the office and when a man fitting his description came out, they approached him.

Jose addressed him. "Señor Font?"

"Yes, what do you want?" he replied, looking very nervous.

"These gentlemen are investigators. They would like to ask you some questions, and if you don't want to get into trouble you had better answer their questions truthfully."

Through Jose they asked, "Were you approached by a man and woman to abduct a child?"

The man looked nervously at Jose who told him, "Answer truthfully and you won't get into trouble. If you don't, the police will be after you."

"Yes, they approached me about two or three weeks ago. I could tell they were foreign and I didn't like them. They wanted me to pick up a child at a school in Bahia Blanca. They offered me a large reward if I would recover their child. I suspected they would kill me rather than pay a reward, so I refused to have anything to do with it."

"Do you know where they are now?"

"No, but a farmer told me that he saw the auto drive towards Bahia Blanca."

Jose thanked him and said that they had kidnapped an important child. He gave him a note with the Grosses' phone number on it and asked him to phone that number if he heard or saw anything of these people. There would be a reward for whoever helps in the recovery of the child.

When Jose explained the conversation to the two others, they congratulated him on thinking about the reward incentive. They went to the little local cantina for lunch and to discuss their findings. While having their lunch, they noticed Renaldo doing a lot of discussing with other men in the cantina. Finally, he came over to them and he told Jose that he has told the others of the reward and that if any of them hear or see anything they were to contact him right away. The workers knew a lot of people on the pampas and they were willing to help find the little boy.

Jose thanked Renaldo and paid for Renaldo's and his friend's drinks and meals as a gesture of appreciation in the hope that they will be able to help in the search.

There wasn't any accommodation in Realico so they drove a hundred kilometers towards Bahia Blanca to a town named General Pico which had a hotel, restaurant and phone. Tomaso and Nicholas had a feeling they were getting closer to the kidnappers. They had found out in doing their previous searches that it was harder for a fugitive to hide in the rural areas than a metropolitan location, which is more insular to local gossip.

Tomaso phoned Adam to report their findings and to let him know where they were. He told Adam about the discussion with Renaldo and of Jose's suggestion of a reward, which seemed to spark some local interest and that if the farmers heard of anything for him to expect a phone call from Renaldo. Adam agreed with Jose's suggestion and he said he would gladly give a good reward to get little Albert back safely.

Adam explained his telephone conversation with Mendel and about hearing what sounded like freight train whistles. He figured that Mendel was phoning from a pay phone in a small community. Tomaso assured Adam that they must be getting close and for him to stay close to the phone; there was a good chance that Adam would get a phone call from Renaldo soon.

"When do you expect the next phone call from Mendel?"

"Probably tomorrow night. He always phones just after dark. Give me your number there in case I have to get in touch with you."

Evidently the reward offer was creating a massive gossip network in the pampas region because word had already arrived in Renaldo about the foreigners. Adam got a phone call from Renaldo that night; first, he wanted to know how much the reward was because the people were asking. Adam told him it was 100,000 pesos. He heard a gasp from the other end, and then Adam asked if there was any information. Renaldo said yes there was and Jose should phone him as soon as possible. He will be at the grain company office where the phone was located and he would stay there until he got the phone call from Jose. Adam immediately phoned Jose at the hotel in the village of General Pico. It seemed like forever for the hotel-keeper to get Jose down from his room to answer the phone. He told Jose to phone Renaldo immediately and that he was waiting at the company phone. Renaldo was quite excited. He explained that a farmer in the village of Torquist, which was about 50 kilometers from Bahia Blanca, spotted the Mercedes auto hidden in a barn on a deserted farm just outside of the town. Jose was to meet the farmer at 10 AM at the town Post Office tomorrow morning to receive directions to the farm.

Chapter 12

THE NEXT MORNING they had to leave before daylight because it was a 300 kilometer drive to Tornquist from General Pico, yet they managed to get some coffee and buns in one of the little villages where they bought diesel fuel for the auto. They arrived a few minutes before ten AM at the Post Office to see a man standing outside the building. Renaldo told Jose to ask for Juan. They looked to see if there were any other persons about, then they drove right up in front of the farmer. Jose got out and approached the man and asked if he was Juan and when the man affirmed this, he asked him to get in the auto so they could talk to him. He hesitated, then got in the back seat alongside of Nicholas who smiled at him. Jose explained that these were two men who are trying to find the kidnappers; then he asked the farmer where they could go to talk and not be seen. The farmer directed Jose to his farm which was about two kilometers from the Post Office. On the way he asked Jose if they had breakfast yet. When Jose told him they had had some coffee, the farmer said, "My wife will make you some breakfast while we talk about the foreigners." Juan explained where the farm is that they were hiding out in; it was about one kilometer further down this same road. As soon as he said this, Jose asked if there was a barn where they could hide the Mercedes. Juan said he would pull his vegetable truck out of the barn right now so they could hide the Mercedes in there. When Jose heard that the kidnappers were just down the road from this farm he didn't want to take a chance on Mendel driving by and spotting the car.

The farmer's wife made them a much appreciated breakfast of bacon, eggs, toast and coffee.

Jose asked Juan how come he had spotted the foreigners and Juan explained that he delivered produce to houses throughout the area and had even sold some produce to that house.

This was just the break that they were waiting for because they had been trying to figure a way to get near the hideout and rescue Albert. It looked like Juan may have given them the clue on how to do it. Juan told them that the man quite often left the house just before dark and heading towards town.

Jose asked him if he had ever delivered some produce just after dark to them and he replied that he had on a few occasions.

The three hunters decided that tonight when Mendel went to town Juan would go up to the house with his produce basket and knock on the door as he had done before, only this time Nicholas will be hidden alongside the front door, gun in hand, Tomaso will creep up to the back of the house to see if he can see Albert in a back room.

Just before dark they all hid in Juan's truck and drove to a farm next to the the Mendels. Tomaso and Nicholas both got out of the truck and headed across the field for the back of the hideout. They checked the barn to see if the Mercedes was there; it wasn't, so they took up their positions one at the front and one at the back of the house. As soon as it was dark they saw the truck stop near the hideout entrance. When Juan went up to the front door Nicholas took position alongside the door, readying himself to leap into the house. Juan knocked on the door several times but there was no answer, so Nicholas carefully pushed the door open.

Juan stuck his head in the house and called out a hello. There was no answer, so Nicholas with his flashlight entered the house; there was evidence of people living there but no one home. He called Tomaso in, and then Tomaso remembered his conversation with Adam when Adam mentioned that Mendel said he was going to let Albert talk to his father tonight. Evidently both the Mendels took Albert into town to phone Adam. They told Juan to get in his truck right away and take it back to his farm. They were going to stay hidden in the house and wait for the Mendels to come back.

It was only a half-hour later that they heard voices approaching the house. They took up positions on either side of the door, flashlights and guns ready. When the door opened Albert was shoved in ahead of them into the dark room. Just as both the Mendels entered, Tomaso and Nicholas shone their flashlights into the faces of the Mendels who immediately pulled guns out of their pockets and started to fire them. Luckily both Tomaso and Nicholas held the flashlights far out with their left hands and their guns in their right hands. Bullets smashed into the wall behind them and with the targets both in the flashlight beam they returned the fire, high enough to miss Albert.

Both the Mendels dropped to the floor, mortally wounded, with shots in the head. Tomaso grabbed a frightened Albert and in broken Spanish told him it was all right. Then he took him outside while Nicholas made sure the Mendels were dead, shot in the face and non-recognizable. They then took Albert to Juan's house in the Mercedes the Mendels were using to give him some food and let Jose explain to him that he was going home tonight.

Jose gave Juan some money for helping them and told him that they will make sure he received some of the reward, especially if he made sure the Mendels were buried in an unmarked grave, maybe out on the back of his ranch, where he would bury one of his horses or cows, and with no police report to mess things up.

As soon as Albert was fed and cleaned up, they took him to town and phoned Adam and Heidi giving two tearful and thankful parents the great news and also saying that they would be home in little over an hour. It was after eleven o'clock at night when they arrived. Everyone was there to greet them, even Jose's family, and they were glad to see their father, and especially Albert, back safe and sound. Heidi gave Albert a nice hot bath and tucked a very happy boy back into his own bed.

All the adults gathered down in the main living room after Jose and Eva took their children home to have their own little celebration.

There were a lot of questions being asked. Both Tomaso and Nicholas described how it was Jose that was the main part of the pursuit. He knew how to talk to the people to get the necessary information and it was he that thought up the idea of the reward, which was the factor that broke the case.

Em asked Tomaso what happened to the Mendels; both Tomaso and Nicholas had previously agreed not to divulge what really happened. They said that the authorities have taken care of the kidnappers and they would probably spend a long time in an Argentine jail. They purposely avoided further conversation on the subject.

The next morning they went for a walk in the rose garden with Adam.

"OK, you two," asked Adam. "What really happened up there? Where are the Mendels?"

Tomaso spoke: "Adam, we had no choice. They would have killed us and Albert. They were firing their guns in all directions around that farm house. We had to fire high enough to avoid hitting Albert in the darkness. They both got hit in the face several times. I doubt if they could have been recognized. We paid the farmer, Juan, to bury them out on his ranch with no marking for a grave. The last thing we need right now is to have an International upset over shooting two Argentine citizens. If the police come around asking questions just say you negotiated a small ransom of 10,000 pesos and they dropped the boy off outside your estate unharmed. Better not say anything to Heidi, just tell her what we said to say and the same for Jose. We and Em and Marie should be leaving as soon as possible tomorrow. The fewer for the police to talk to, the better."

There was a big celebration dinner that night. Adam gave generous cheques to Tomaso and Nicholas, more than enough to cover all their expenses and payment for their work.

When he spoke to Em about paying him for his expenses, Em just laughed and said; "Adam, Marie and I were planning to come over here to see you two anyway. I'm sorry it had to be for this reason but we are both very happy everything turned out all right. As for the expenses, I'm writing them off as a Directors' meeting, so you are paying for it in your share of the profit, like you'll do when you and the family come to see Marie and me. By the way, I have left the latest statements of the Company on your desk; we are still making lots of money because there are more airlines now using our service all over West Africa."

"Thanks Em, you know, when we first met you, you asked Frieda a question. Can you recall what it was?"

They were grinning at each other. "Yes, I think I know what you are getting at and the answer is, we are getting married, next month. Your invitation is in the mail. I'd like you to be my best man and Marie is going to ask Heidi to be her maid of honour."

"I'm sure glad to hear that, and I know Heidi will be very pleased."

The next morning, after much hugging and kissing, Jose drove all the visitors up to Buenos Aires so they could catch their flights home. The Grosses couldn't thank them enough for their help and consolation.

On November 15, 1955, the Grosses received a letter from Em which included the invitations to the wedding and airline tickets for all three. The wedding date was set for November 30, 1955. It was to be held at the palace, the same location as their wedding had been. There was a letter in with the invitation advising them that they would be put up at the palace and that everything had been taken care of for transportation and accommodation.

Jose drove them up the Airport in Buenos Aires. They were to fly on Lufthansa, so Heidi and Adam both wondered what kind of plane Lufthansa would be using. When they walked out of the passenger terminal and saw the plane they started to laugh. Some of the passengers who witnessed the scene thought maybe it was a nervous laugh about flying in a plane. In 1955 there weren't that many people flying yet, most were going by boat or train, but it was the plane that made them laugh. It was a Condor painted white. Albert asked them why they were laughing; they told him they would explain it all when they got aboard. They explained that it was the same plane that brought them to Argentina from Europe many years ago. They enjoyed the flight especially as they watched Albert while flying over the scenic route.

Just before they got to Rio the captain came back to use the washroom. As he went by the Grosses he gave Heidi a nod and smile. Later on, the stewardess said the captain had invited all of them to come up to the flight deck. When they entered the deck the captain got out of his seat and invited Heidi to take his seat, but before doing so he introduced himself as Captain Bruno Wagner. Smiling at Heidi, he said, "I was once your co-pilot on one of the first Condors. I'd be pleased if you will take command for a few moments."

Adam was smiling and shook hands with the captain who said, "It's a pleasure to see you again, sir."

Albert, the co-pilot, engineer and navigator all had looks of bewilderment.

Heidi asked the navigator for the heading. She corrected the plane's direction, then turned the control back to the captain, thanking him and saying that it was a pleasure to fly with him.

When they got back to their seats Adam had to explain to the child who was full of questions. He told Albert the story of how his mother was once a pilot who flew these very planes with that captain.

One day in 1960 a car drove up to the hacienda gate. A well dressed man got out of the car and strolled up to the gate. He told Jose that he was looking for the Grosses and gave his card to Jose to be presented to Adam or Heidi.

The card showed that his name was Peter Wasmuth, President and Chairman of Lufthansa Airlines, Bonn, Germany.

When Jose showed the card to Adam he asked, "Do you want to see this person?"

Adam said,"Yes, please show him in and tell Heidi to please come in from the garden, that we have company."

Adam greeted Peter at the front door with a warm embrace and double hand-shake and then led him into the living room. Adam and Peter were standing in the living room waiting for Heidi to freshen up after working in the garden.

She had no idea who the guest was until she entered the room where she exclaimed, "Peter!" with a big smile, giving him a hug. "What a pleasant surprise. Have you had breakfast yet?"

"I had an early breakfast in Buenos Aires, but I'll settle for a cup of coffee."

Heidi said;" Let's go out on the garden terrace so we can relax and hear all about your life since we last saw you."

Eva brought the coffee carafe and cups out to the terrace. Heidi introduced Peter to Eva, explaining to Eva that he was a good friend from Germany.

Before Heidi could ask, "What's new?" to Peter, Adam said to Heidi, "Peter has got my old job. He's the President of Lufthansa. I am sure he has lots to tell us about the firm. And Peter, how long can you stay? We want you to be our guest here, there is so much we have to catch up on about the firm and Germany?"

"Well, I can stay a couple of days. I have to get back to a place in Africa called Rinsque. I have a meeting scheduled for two days from now with a Sheik there. I have to negotiate the price of fuel for the airline. Evidently he is the head of the company that supplies fuel for all the airlines using North Africa." He said this with a smile, knowing that Heidi and Adam were good friends of Em.

"What is happening in Germany? We read in the papers about some of the political changes, but how is it recovering from the war?"

"Well Adam, you'll have to excuse me, I still want to call you both by your original names. I know you have a son, Albert, but why can't you re-register as Albert and Frieda Wirth, citizens of Argentina? The war has long been over and forgotten. You could even come back to Germany and live a comfortable life. It appears you are well fixed financially; think of Albert's future, I am sure he would be better off eventually even though he has roots here."

"Yes Peter, you have hit on something we have been discussing lately."

"Tell you what I'll do. I'll give you all passes for the airline. Come to Bonn, be my guests, then you all can see for yourselves the new Germany. At least take me up on my offer to make a holiday of it."

He continued, "By the way, you both will be interested in the new type transports we are using. The one I came down on is a Boeing 707. It's a fantastic jet plane, you both will love it. It is very fast and can go much further than the prop planes could in one hop."

"Peter, how come you know so much about us, we haven't seen each other in years?"

"Well Al, I mean Adam, do you remember a young pilot named Tomaso Sklarenko?"

"Yes, we sure do. He was one of the people who helped us recover Albert from the kidnappers. What about him?"

"Well, he is now a captain flying 707s for Lufthansa. He does the Africa and South America run; he might even be your pilot when you fly to Germany," he said with a grin, knowing he was taking for granted that they will go to Germany.

"I don't know if we would be welcome back in Germany. After all, Heidi and I stole the Condor when we escaped."

"It is a good thing you did take the Condor. If you hadn't, it would have been destroyed in the raid on the Flying Club. All the other Condors were destroyed in Norway or France where they were used against Allied shipping. All we had left was a few ancient Junker 52s and the Condor you saved by getting it out of Germany. No, Al, you two are heroes of Lufthansa. If you hadn't saved the Condor there might never have been a Lufthansa again."

"The people of Germany want to forget the war. It was like having a bad dream. There were terrible losses of life and property. I lost everything, and had to start all over again. Even my wife and child were killed in the air raids. For two years I was a lost soul, and then I heard about the white Condor down here in Argentina. I managed to get a couple of politicians interested in starting Lufthansa up again. They wrote to the Argentina Government and requested the Condor be released back to Germany and thanked them for storing it for them. I and an ex-Lufthansa pilot that flew the Condors, flew it back to Germany. That sheik friend of yours said because you were a friend of his and if we agreed to use his service for Lufthansa, he would write off the cost of the fuel we used to get the Condor back. That helped to get Lufthansa back on its feet again.

"We have planes flying all over the world now. I'd like very much for you two to come and see what you created by saving that Condor and what the new Germany looks like. It is a republic now; the people have some say. No more dictator and secret police, and you could run for public office and probably get in because you are both well known. Or if you are financially well fixed you could get a chateau in France or a villa on the Mediterranean. Albert could get his education at one of the schools in Switzerland or any university in Europe. Think about it--at least take a trip there to size things up. I think you will be pleased with the changes. Let me know when you want to come and I'll make the arrangements for you."

Peter stayed for two days and young Albert got to meet his Uncle Peter. There were lots of things to discuss, but Peter never mentioned about the man-hunt for the kidnappers or about the story of two other people in the plane when they flew the Condor out of Germany. He wanted them all to start a new life with a fresh start.

Chapter 13

IN THE SUMMER of 1962, Adam and Heidi decided to change their names back to Albert and Frieda Wirth, along with young Albert being registered as Albert Wirth. Albert Senior went back to being called Al again, making things less confusing. When it was all explained to young Albert he accepted the change of his name, especially when he was told the story of his mother and father as pilots on the German airline and that his mother was a famous aviatrix.

It was Jose, Eva and their children that found it the hardest to adjust to the new names. They had only known them as the Gross family.

It was that year that Al and Frieda decided to contact Peter and arrange for them to go back to Germany for a trip. Only a few days later they received their passes for First Class on a 707 leaving from Buenos Aires to Bonn, Germany. They wired Peter and told him when they were leaving. A tearful Jose drove them to the airport in Buenos Aires and bid them a please return soon, knowing that there could be plans for Al and the family to move to Europe.

Neither Frieda nor Al had ever seen a jet transport and they were amazed at its size and accommodations. Before boarding they were entertained in the special lounge for celebrities and then went aboard after every one else had boarded. Albert was very excited at flying in a jet plane; he had only flown in the Condor. Both Frieda and Al realized that he had been missing a lot by living a secluded life in Argentina; it was going to be interesting to see how he took to Germany.

The speed of takeoff and climb made Al and Frieda grin at each other. This was the jet age and they were both enjoying it.

When the plane reached its cruising level, which only took a few minutes, the head flight attendant came up to Frieda to ask her if she would like to see the flight deck. Of course she would--she was itching to see it.

When she entered the deck the attendant closed the door. The pilot turned smiling--it was Tomaso! She rushed over to him and gave him a big kiss. He hadn't told the co-pilot who was aboard, the co-pilot was wondering what was going on, and then Tomaso introduced Frieda Wirth, the world famous aviatrix to his co-pilot who now knew why she was on the flight deck. Tomaso asked the co-pilot to give his seat to Frieda, which he gladly did.

Tomaso said to Frieda: "It's a little faster to response than the Condor but hold lightly on to the control wheel. I'm going to switch off the auto pilot and we will both fly it. All set?"

She gave a nod and was amazed at her ease in moving the controls of this monster. He gradually let her take control, and she held it steady on course, having to give it slight corrections without any difficulty. The co-pilot stood to watch this woman pilot legend fly the plane with absolute ease. He was very impressed to meet and watch this famous person take his seat and fly the plane as though she were the captain. Reluctantly, she finally gave the seat back to him. She thanked Tomaso and gave him a kiss on the cheek. He asked her to send Al and Albert up forward when you get back.

When she got back to her seat Al said quietly to her, "I knew when you took over. I could feel the plane's motion change." She sent her two men up to the flight deck. Albert was excited about seeing the flight deck of this big airplane and even more when he realized it was uncle Tomaso who was the captain, and then Al was given his opportunity to fly this wonderful machine, much to his and Albert's delight. It was a wonderful experience; the Wirth family was flying back to Germany and, unlike the original flight, this was a happy and joyous occasion.

Before they landed at Rinsque, Tomaso had radioed ahead to the Lufthansa office instructing them to let Em know when they would arrive.

When they arrived at Rinsque, Em was there to greet them. They had planned on staying for a few days with Uncle Em, the Sheik, and Princess Marie.

Em's young chauffeur drove the women to shopping then he took Albert on a sightseeing trip of the area which he enjoyed very much. The men had some very important business to catch up on.

This time Karl Andersen was there. He had aged considerably as it had been twenty–three years since they all met to hold that original meeting that started the REAAFCO Company. They had all prospered from the company and were here now to discuss its future.

Karl said, "Gentlemen, I am going to have to sell you my shares. My health isn't too good and I'd like to retire to my homeland, Denmark."

Em said, "Karl, I'm very sorry to hear you are having a health problem. I know I speak also for Al about your situation. OK, gentlemen, shall we work out the present standing of our shares in the business?"

Em had the current statements on hand. The calculation of liquid cash on hand was easy; it was shown on the statement. The value of the real estate holdings was a little more difficult; it would require an appraiser to handle the valuation.

Em worked out the total cash on hand in the company's Swiss account, divided it by three and showed it to the other two members. They shook their heads in approval.

Karl said that a transfer to his Swiss account of his third cash share would be appreciated and he would accept whatever the appraiser determined as the real estate value, then they could transfer his share to his account when they see fit.

Em poured out three glasses of Scotch, passed them out and said, "Here's to the best partnership there ever was. May you, Karl, find peace and happiness in your retirement. Salute!"

They took Karl to the airport the next day and wished him the best of luck and thanked him for being their partner.

When they got back to the Palace, Em said, "Let's head for the office. This wake is on me and I guess there are some things we should discuss about the future of our business."

Em poured the drinks and then he said, "You know, Karl realized if he insisted on a complete cash settlement it could have put a crimp in our business. Our holdings are quite substantial. We could have met the demand, but there is something else we have to consider and that's why we have to talk. With just the two of us owning the business we are more flexible to look into other investments. We are piling up cash in the Swiss account; it is time to start making the cash flow work for us."

"What do you suggest, Em?"

"We should place the cash flow into accounts that pay interest on our chequing account. The funds will be there to meet our payment schedule, but we will earn interest and still be liquid. The banks are getting heavy demands for industrial funds and domestic funds for mortgages; they need our money and should be willing to negotiate an interest rate for our account. Also, we should invest some disposable cash into sound investments. The industrial world is going through a tremendous boom with the expansion of industry and it needs money, lots of it, and we have it. All we have to do is make it work for us by investing in 'blue chip' investments."

"Em, I've been out of touch with the industrial world for several years. I'll have to leave it up to you to get this idea rolling. It sounds great and I'm all for it. On our return trip from Germany, we will go into the financial investment idea a lot deeper. By the way, we are talking about going back to Germany to live, it all depends on how things work out on this trip. We have to think of Albert's future and what is best for him."

"That's good thinking, Al. Now is the time to make a move back to Europe while properties are still low in price and while Albert is still in his younger years of education and friends. It'll be easier for him now, but if you wait until he has a girl friend it could be hard on him."

Al wired Peter to let him know what flight they would be on. They left the day after Al had his business talk with Em. The Rinsque airport was still used by Lufthansa and a few of the other airlines. There were two other jet transports sitting on the tarmac getting serviced. Their Lufthansa flight was ready to take off as soon as they got aboard, the plane taxied out to the paved runway and was airborne in seconds. Again they were treated as celebrities and enjoyed the flying in this fast, wonderful plane.

It was a smooth five-hour flight to Tripoli where the plane was refueled by the same firm as in Rinsque, the REAAFCO Company. Frieda noticed this and said, "That service firm seems to have a toehold on the North Africa business for selling fuel to the airlines. I wonder who is behind it?"

As she mentioned this, Al smiled. Laughing, she asked, "Did I say something funny? What is it?"

"I couldn't tell you before but remember all those business meetings Em and I have had? Well, guess who owns that Company."

"Em?"

"Yes, and us."

"What do you mean 'us'?"

"Remember the famous trip we took to Rinsque, when we got married, and the fellow who was my best man, Karl Andersen? Em proposed the three of us form a company to supply Lufthansa and some other companies with fuel. Karl had the oil franchise, I had the say for Lufthansa and Em acted as our go between and manager. He handled all the setting up and administration of the business through a lawyer friend of his in Switzerland."

With a look of complete surprise she replied, "Well I'll be damned. You're telling me that we are rich?"

"Yes rich, but not filthy rich, just comfortably rich, but getting richer. This is another reason we have to take a look at Europe, as well as for Albert's future."

"You had a premonition of all this on that first flight we took to Africa, didn't you? And right now you are smiling that same funny smile that I asked you about on that wonderful trip."

"Yes, I had a strong feeling that something good was going to come out of our meeting with Em. I guess it is a feeling of lift one gets when they rise up the ladder of success and meet people of importance. Something in the brain clicks into place expanding one's horizons and allowing a person to advance in business or society. Em and I have bought Karl's share of the business. He had to sell to us because of his failing health. Em and I are now more able to look into other means of investing. We are going to have more frequent meetings, another reason we should move to Europe. I'm glad I finally can divulge the information about REAAFCO. No more worries about trying to hide our thoughts and interests from the Gestapo."

"What have you planned for on this trip to Bonn?"

"Well, after listening to what Peter had to say about the changes in Europe I thought it might be a good idea if we rent a car and travel around Europe and size up things. Check out a good place for us and Albert to live, maybe even southern Spain, seeing that we now speak Spanish and understand their way of life after Argentina. We will see. It all depends on how we make out travelling around Europe and eventually the friends we make in our new start. Let's be positive and look forward to an exciting new life."

The jet plane was so fast that they were in Bonn before they could do any further planning. Albert was fascinated with the view of Europe and the number of buildings. Frieda and Al realized that Albert had been living a secluded life in Bahia Blanca and this trip will be good for him.

Peter was at the Lufthansa terminal to meet them. After greeting them he drove them to his home on the outskirts of Bonn. He asked them if they had eaten and they said they had a nice luncheon on board the plane, so he said: "Great, I know a nice restaurant where we can have supper after you have had a chance to freshen up."

Frieda and Al, when flying for Lufthansa, never had the opportunity to see much of Bonn. It was a quiet little city on the Rhine and hadn't developed into much more than a tourist place before the war. It was now the capital of the Federal Republic of Germany; it had been rebuilt after the war and was now a bustling city. One thing Al and Frieda noticed was the vast numbers of Volkswagen Beetle cars. Before the war very few people could afford an auto.

Al mentioned to Peter about the change in affluence.

"Yes Al, when West Germany changed its type of government to the republic system, it started to flourish immediately. The citizens liked having more say in the operation of their government than what they have had through two wars and an old feudal system. I wanted all of you to come and see the new Germany. I strongly recommend you take a rented car trip throughout Germany. I believe you will be pleased at what you will see."

The next day Al and Frieda opened an account in a West German bank, and then they rented a Mercedes sedan and obtained highway maps from the auto rental agency. That night after supper, Peter laid out a suggested route for them and he also suggested for them to be open minded about changing their itinerary. They will want to make the most of seeing the New Germany.

The next morning they packed their luggage into the auto and left early in the morning after saying farewell to Peter. Instead of heading south as they intended to do, they decided to visit Dusseldorf to see if there were any changes there and to do a little reminiscing. It was where they first met and they wanted to show Albert where his mother used to live. The hospital was still there but where she used to live had been rebuilt. There were still scars from the war; it was depressing so they just did a quick tour around the city, stopped for lunch and then carried on down to Cologne for their first night's stop at an inn with a tavern.

This was all new to young Albert. He liked the heavy German sausage meal and the way they cooked the potatoes with lots of cheese. After supper they stayed in the tavern talking to locals who came in to have their beer. They gave Albert a soft drink called Coca Cola that had just been franchised into Germany, while they had their beer. The people didn't want to talk about the war, they wanted to discuss their future and what had been accomplished, and they appeared enthusiastic about the economy.

The next day, after having a good night's rest, they headed for Frankfurt. They drove along the picturesque Rhine Valley pointing out the historic sites to Albert in German. They had kept and taught Albert their native tongue along with some French and of course he learned Spanish while going to school in Bahia Blanca. It was very exciting for Albert to see the historic castles and read about them in the travel brochures. He gave his parents a running commentary from the brochures as they drove along the Rhine Valley.

When they got to the town of Mainz they turned off the Rhine Valley and up the main Valley to Frankfurt, where they got rooms for the three of them at a large hotel and their supper in the hotel dining room. It was late when they arrived so they went to bed right after eating.

The next day they headed back down the main valley to the Rhine, following it into Switzerland. The country they had been driving through was fairly mountainous but when they got to Switzerland Albert and Frieda were awe-struck by the high mountains and their beauty. They stayed their first night in Switzerland at a hotel down in the business district of Zurich amongst the banks. Al wanted to meet the manager and get an up to date statement of his account. The receptionist had kind of a snooty attitude when she observed this family who wanted to see the manager.

She asked, "May I ask who you are?"

"Yes, I am Albert Wirth from Argentina. This is my family and I'm the co-owner of the REAAFCO Corporation."

She wasn't in there long and came out with a different attitude and announced that the manager will see you soon. He was just finishing with a customer. Whoever was in seeing the manager was ushered out right away. The manager came up and shook hands with Al, and then Al introduced him to his family. They were invited into the office where Al requested the information he wanted.

The manager looked at his watch and said, "Herr Wirth, I'd be honoured if you and your family would join me at my Club for lunch. We can go there in my auto. I'll have the secretary prepare your statements and they will be ready for you right after lunch."

The Club was a Golf Club in the summer and a ski resort during the winter. The clubhouse was a chalet built overlooking a valley with a panoramic spectacular scene of the golf course and up onto the surrounding high mountains.

"Are you still living in Argentina, Herr Wirth?"

"Yes we are, but we are taking a tour looking for a good place to live in Europe, one that will be good for Albert with regard to education and enjoyment for him."

"May I make a suggestion?"

"Yes by all means. It has been several years since we've lived in Europe. We would appreciate any help we could get regarding a move back here."

"Well, as you realize a lot of countries in Europe are in a vast state of reconstruction. It's going to be costly and will take several years to pay for it. There are two places that were not devastated by the war, Switzerland and Liechtenstein. Both these countries have tax benefits and good financial institutions. You could purchase property in them making you a citizen. Also, you could purchase your main home in another city like Friedrichshafen, only fifty kilometers from Liechtenstein in Germany, on beautiful Lake Constance, where Albert can attend school. I suggest you look at these places on your tour."

After having an enjoyable luncheon and conversation they went back to the bank, got their statements, and thanked the manager for his hospitality and suggestions. They left immediately and drove the seventy-five kilometers to Vaduz, the capital of Liechtenstein, where they got rooms at an inn. They stayed two days touring the country and talking to the people; finally they went to the government office and received all the information regarding immigration. At first, the immigration officer was not receptive, but when Al explained that they were there at the suggestion of the bank manager, the attitude changed. Evidently one could apply but only those with the appropriate financial means would be accepted. Everyone here was rich and they wanted to keep it that way.

After sizing up Liechtenstein, they took the bank manager's advice and drove up to Friedrichshafen. This city was the center of early German aviation. It was where the famous zeppelins were made and stored, also it was where the giant Dornier DOX flying boat was built and tested on Lake Constance. This was the plane that Al piloted across the Atlantic. Because of his experience flying the DOX, Hitler had singled Al out at that first meeting and eventually appointed him President of Lufthansa.

They stayed in a hotel in Friedrichshafen for three days, going to the museums and touring this famous aviation city. On the second night they decided this was the place they wanted to live in, so on the third day they had a real estate agent show them some nice estate homes in the best residential section of the city. After inspecting several, they picked out an estate property that had been built by an industrialist before the last war. Like their place in Bahia Blanca, it had large grounds and a caretaker's residence at its gated entrance. The original owners had passed away just after the war and the heirs of the estate found it didn't meet their desire for a more modern house. They were willing to sell it for a very reasonable price during this time of a glut on the market of old, expensive homes. Frieda loved this old mansion; her memory of living in Germany was, first, the little shoebox apartment in Dusseldorf, and then their honeymoon apartment in Berlin. She immediately realized this could be made into the grand mansion that it was originally intended to be. She told Al that this was the place she wanted to be--it was their home in Germany. They bought it and then contacted a contractor to redecorate the whole house and appointed the real estate agent to oversee that the work was carried out as in the contract.

Before leaving Argentina they had their names changed back to the Wirths, so their passports showed them as still being Argentines.

When they got things settled in Friedrichshafen they went back to Liechtenstein, applied for citizenship there, got their Liechtenstein passports and bought a chalet at a ski resort. Before leaving both places they took photos of them with the cameras they had brought for the tour.

When they had finished their arrangements, they headed back to Bonn. It took them two days to travel back through the Rhine Valley. They were anxious to tell Peter that they were going to be living in Germany once more and show him the pictures of their houses.

Peter was very pleased that his good friends had decided to come back to Germany.

They showed him the pictures of their purchases and expressed their appreciation for his help in convincing them to return. They explained that they had better get back to Argentina to finalize their affairs there. They would return to Friedrichshafen as soon as the decorators were finished and the mansion was ready to move into, then they could get Albert enrolled in a school there.

Tomaso was again their pilot flying the Boeing 707 to Rinsque. They told him about their purchases and when they mentioned Friedrichshafen he said, " You couldn't have picked a better place to live in. If I were retiring, that's the place I would choose. I have been there several times to see the aviation museum and flying events. They have a good flying club there and you both should join it. It might be a good idea to pick up one of the aviation magazines that advertises different types of planes for sale; there are some great bargains, such as those DC3s that were built for the American brass to fly in during the war. They're stored up in the California high desert at a place called Mojave. They should be in good shape and I hear they are going for low prices."

When they landed at Rinsque, they thanked Tomaso for all the help he had given them, and they said they were thinking about what he said about those executive DC3s and were going to look into it. They gave him their address in Friedrichshafen and asked him to please look them up.

Frieda asked him if he was married yet? He smiled and said that it was going to happen soon. Frieda said, "When are you planning to do it?"

"Well, Elke is a flight attendant. We are trying to arrange it in November when we both can get off."

"That's great, Tomaso. Our place at Friedrichshafen should be ready by then. We're inviting you use our place for your wedding and honeymoon. It will be a great way to celebrate the opening of our home there. I know Al agrees because Em did the same thing for us and it is one way we can show our appreciation for what you did for us."

They spent two days with uncle Em and Aunty Marie. The women talked about the planning of Tomaso's and Elke's wedding. Marie and Em would come up a few days in advance to help with the arrangements. Al and Em had a lot of things to discuss about their business adventure.

"Well Al, it sounds like you spent a lot of money on this trip. I'm glad to hear it, so now we have to get busy investing to make ourselves even richer so you can pay all those bills you are going to accumulate."

Al related his meeting with the Swiss banker and suggested that it looked like they could get some good financial advice about investing through their contacts there.

While discussing their business opportunities, Al said, "There is one thing I noticed travelling in Europe. There seems to be a building boom going on. I imagine in Europe it is mostly reconstruction after the war, but in North America I imagine it is similar to the one that came after the First World War, a baby boom. It could create a large demand for electrical products. How about observing the shares of firms like General Electric of the USA and the Phillips Company? I have a feeling their stock could explode in value."

"Good suggestion, Al. Remember that lawyer friend in Switzerland? Well, I'm going to give him a call and see if he can put us onto a good stockbroker who is reliable. I have the same feeling as you, Al. I think there is going to be a considerable demand for products. We hit it lucky because of the war, now if we are prudent our fortunes will multiply considerably. I'll give you a phone call when you get home to Argentina to let you know how I made out."

The Wirths caught the next flight going to Buenos Aires. Al had phoned Jose to let him know when they would arrive, so he could pick them up at the airport.

During the flight home Al and Frieda discussed what to do about Jose and Eva because it is evident they should sell their place at Bahia Blanca. They decided to buy a home for Jose and Eva at a place of their choosing, probably in Bahia Blanca, because their friends and relatives were there. Also they agreed to send money each month to them to carry them over until Jose got a job.

Jose was at the airport and gave them a warm welcome. He was very glad to see them. On the drive home they discussed about Jose's family and about Casa Del Mar. Without any forethought, it just struck Al to ask Jose if he had ever considered starting his own business.

"Yes I have because I always knew that you people would someday want to go back to your country. I have thought of it many times."

"What would you like to do, Jose?"

"I'd like to have my own store selling farm produce."

"Any idea of how much you would need to set up a proper store to sell not only farm produce but all groceries?"

"No, I have never been able to consider such an enterprise."

"Will you look into how much it will cost to set up a good grocery store and let me know as soon as possible?"

"Yes, Senor!" Jose became so excited and anxious to get home they thought he was going to make the auto become air-borne.

Eva and the children were very pleased to see them home again. Eva, with her woman's instinct, felt there was something different about the Wirths and she was a little quiet. She had a nice meal all ready for them and served it with a concerned look on her face.

Evidently Jose, that evening, had told Eva about the discussion he had with Senor Al. The next day she was a happy smiling Eva again. They had discussed their future several times before and it looked like Al had hit on the thing they really wanted to do, become merchants in Bahia Blanca.

Frieda asked Al how come he came up the solution for Jose and Eva.

"Well, I suddenly thought while he was driving us home, what would I want if I were in his shoes and maybe he has been thinking about an idea to become independent. It just kind of blurted out of me."

"It's a very good idea. It appears they are both happy about it. I'm glad you thought of it and it should make our parting here a lot happier one."

Two days later Jose drove Al into town and showed him the store he wanted. He also had pamphlets of fixtures and equipment he would need, along with prices. Jose said his relatives would give a hand helping to install the shelving and equipment.

Al told him to go ahead, lease the store and order the equipment. It was a little more than he had expected but in the long run it was probably better than sending them money every month until he got a job. Also there was the sale of Casa Del Mar which should more than cover all the costs. As for the two Mercedes, one was already in Jose's name and probably the other would go with the sale of the mansion to a rich buyer. Maybe even some day, Jose might be able to buy Casa Del Mar when he became successful.

At the end of September the agent in Friedrichshafen phoned to tell them their house was finished and that it looked wonderful. There were several rich people wanting to buy it.

On October 15 Casa Del Mar was sold. Thanks to Eva and Jose's good caretaking it sold quickly for a good price. Also Al persuaded the new owners to keep Jose and Eva living in the caretaker's house.

A few pieces of expensive antique furniture they kept and arranged to be packed and shipped to their new home in Germany.

On October 20 they visited a very busy Jose at the opening of Jose's market. He and Eva were so busy they barely had time to say farewell with quick hugs and sad goodbyes. It was a lot easier than what Al and Frieda had originally anticipated. They were glad for them and wished them well. The new owner of Casa Del

Mar drove them to the airport. A lot better future loomed ahead of them than when they had arrived here several years ago.

While waiting for their flight in Buenos Aires, Al bought an aviation magazine; it was something for him to read on the trip.

When they got settled down after the take-off, they were discussing about how things turned out with Jose and Eva. They both felt very relieved that things worked out so well for these two friends of theirs and started to discuss Albert's future in Germany.

Frieda said," I think we made our return to Germany just in time."

"How come?"

"Well, Albert is now sixteen. He is tall, blond like his father, good looking and I began to notice some of those dark-eyed beauties in Argentina doing a double take on him. If we stayed any longer there was a good chance he would fall in love with one of them there, and that would have created a family problem if we wanted to make this move. Being a woman, I was more aware of the female attraction towards him. That's why I pushed for this change in our lives. I knew what would happen if we stayed much longer, we'd be stuck there, then his chances of getting a higher education in Europe could be lost."

"Was it your female drive that attracted you to me?"

"Yes, you're damned right. It was your good looks and sure as heck not your money. Of course all nurses after a few years on the job start looking for a husband. In my case along came this good-looking pilot and I nailed him. Fortunately, he became the president of Lufthansa and eventually led to this wonderful life we are living. Also because he had a funny feeling about his future with Swiss bank accounts."

In the magazine there was an article about the sale of War Asset aircraft and it gave the address of the agency in Washington D.C. U.S.A. that was handling the sale of the aircraft. There were several pictures of different type planes describing their condition and specs. Reading the article, Al got the old urge to fly again; he started to visualize having one of the deluxe executive-equipped DC3s and flying it all over Europe and North Africa. Maybe someday…

They stayed briefly in Rinsque to visit with uncle Em and Aunty Marie, who were surprised how Albert has sprouted up in the last few months and how his voice has become deeper. He was now a young man.

Em showed Al the shares the company had bought in the companies that Al had suggested on the previous trip. A month after the purchase the stocks were split to twice their value. The broker in Switzerland was phoning continually trying to sell them more stocks. Em agreed to phone Al before doing any more investing. They agreed to play the market cautiously, just play with the winnings and not dip into the original capital. Al was going to keep his ears open in the Liechtenstein and Zurich places of business. The stock market is a gambling business and it pays to have good advice and knowledge of what is going on in the market. One thing they agreed on was to diversify their investments, not put too many eggs in one basket; they were investing a lot of money and could lose a lot in investing too much on one stock.

After having a pleasant visit with Em and Marie, they caught a flight for Munich, and then they taxied to their home in Friedrichshafen. The next day Al phoned the local Mercedes dealer and requested they send a black, four-door sedan, fully serviced, to their residence along with all the necessary papers to complete the sale. They would need an auto to get around while finishing the purchases they needed for this wonderful home. All three of them were pleased with this mansion; it was situated up on a slope above Lake Constance, high enough to give an unobstructed view of the lake and the surrounding area.

Within two weeks they had the place ready for Elke and Tomaso's wedding. Frieda sent a letter to Tomaso advising him everything was set for the wedding, and pleaded to let her know when and how many will be attending.

During the first week in Friedrichshafen Al and Albert drove all over the area checking out good private schools that Albert could attend and still live at home. There were three they inspected and Al let Albert select the one he wanted to attend. The one he chose had a good language curriculum of Latin, French, German and English. Its science laboratory was well equipped and the instructors they met seemed friendly and not too stiff. Albert would be spending at least two years here before going to the University in Munich.

Tomaso's and Elke's wedding went off smoothly, thanks to help from Aunty Marie. Most of the people attending were involved in the aviation business, friends of Tomsso and Elke, pilots with their wives and flight attendants, some with their spouses, even Peter Wasmuth, the President of the company was there.

It was like the gathering of the eagles, a lot of reminiscing and airplane talk. Al was glad Peter was there so some of the older pilots and Al could be company for Em.

The pilots all knew of the great aviatrix Frieda Wirth and during the wedding dinner when the toasts were being presented, Peter gave one to the world's greatest woman pilot – Frieda.

During the dancing and after the dinner Elke introduced the beautiful blonde friend who was her maid of honour to Peter Wasmuth. After doing so she gave Frieda a sly wink and lifted her eyebrows as if to say, I hope it works.

Frieda thought, "Uh-oh, another wedding in the making."

Al talked to several of the pilots that have flown the DC3s as he was anxious to hear what they had to say about the famous transport plane. They all said it was a wonderful plane and if they had the money they would buy one.

It was discussions like these with the pilots that convinced him he should buy one of the executive DC3s before they were all sold, or there was very little selection of ones in good condition. The next business day he phoned the office handling the sale of the planes in Washington D.C. and found out that they had a list of the planes for sale and where they could be seen. After receiving and reading the brochure about the DC 3s and their prices, they decided to go to California to look at them as they were stored up in the high desert. They would like to pick out one in good condition and if they were lucky go for a test flight in it.

They contacted a woman housekeeper to live at the house and take care of Albert while they flew to California to check out the planes. They booked flights all the way to the Los Angeles Airport where they chartered a small plane to fly them up to the desert town of Mojave. The charter pilot told them he would land at the Mojave Airport near the stored planes and he would radio ahead for the manager there to meet them at the DC3s as he was bringing a customer to look at them. On the flight up he told them that he flew the DC3s over the hump into Burma during the war and that he envied them being able to buy one, especially the Executive models. He said, "They are luxury!" They asked him to wait to fly them back to Los Angeles.

He said, "Tell you what, I'll check you out on one if you want me to. The manager probably hasn't got a license to do so. I've got an instructor ticket so I can check you out. Can either of you fly a plane or have flown one before?"

They both smiled at him and replied yes, a bit.

"You know I have a strong feeling about you two. I'm sure I know you, Madam. I think you are the German aviatrix, Frieda. I've been an aviation buff ever since I built model planes in the thirties. Am I right?"

"Yes, you are right. She not only flew the Messerschmitt Racer but she was a captain who flew the big Condors all over Europe. We sure appreciate your offer to check us out. That is very kind of you. By the way, I was also a captain on Lufthansa and I'm pleased to have you as my instructor."

"Holy cow! I've never had top people in aviation as students before; you've just made my day."

After he landed, he taxied up to the Executive DC3s where the manager was there to greet them and let them into the one in the best condition. The pilot checked the fuel gauge and announced that there was plenty of fuel. He asked the manager to give him a hand at taking the covers off the engines and the lock bars on the rudder and elevators. When the manager balked at getting the plane ready, the pilot said, "Look, these people have come all the way from Europe to see this plane. Don't stand around with your finger up your ass. Help me get it ready for a test flight. I'll sign for it."

It must have been in use recently because the batteries were in good condition and the engines started easily. Both Frieda and Al did an external check before the pilot warmed up the engines. This was a real luxury plane; it had everything on board that one could think of to make it a luxury craft: the seats and upholstery was of the best material and it reeked of opulence.

When Frieda and Al joined the pilot he said, "By the way, my name is Wilbur Wright."

Al introduced himself and said, "Are you related to the famous Wright Brothers?"

"I don't think so. My dad was a pilot in World War l and was always keenly interested in aviation and having the last name of Wright he decided to name me Wilbur. He taught me how to fly before I could drive a car."

Both Frieda and Al laughed and Al said, "Frieda was flying planes years before she learned how to drive a car."

They both liked Wilbur; he was a good down-to-earth person who would do anything for a fellow aviator. He was a special breed of human that would rather fly than do anything else and could fly any type of plane.

After completing the checklist he taxied the DC3 out to the runway. There was no Control Tower at this field, so he asked them to help do a visual check of the air to make sure it was clear for takeoff. When they gave the OK he lined the plane up with the runway and gave it full throttle. Being lightly loaded, the plane picked up speed very quickly and lifted off smoothly after a short run for such a large plane. Wilbur told them about how he had to fly heavy loads into small fields in Burma. They had to carry their own fuel in as part of the cargo, then take off again with a full load of wounded and the plane's full tanks from the same small fields.

"For instance, this field we just took off from is at 3,500 feet elevation. Give this baby 20 degrees flap and full throttle, I swear it could lift a tank up. Now I take it both of you use the metric system. OK, see that pouch behind my seat? There is an envelope in it containing metric decals to put on the instruments. Al, if you will put them on the co-pilot instruments I can start to give you both instructions."

They flew over the Mojave Desert for three hours with Wilbur giving both Al and Frieda instruction, and then turning the plane over to each to take their turn in the co-pilot's position.

One of the things Wilbur did to prove to them how good this plane was: he turned off one engine and flew level on only one engine. That did it. They were actually sold on the plane when they first saw inside it, but after enjoying flying it and realizing how good it was, they are sold. Wilbur let Frieda bring it in for a landing giving her instruction but not touching the controls.

Frieda taxied the plane up to the manager's field office and they all went inside. Al asked the manager if he had all the papers for the plane as well as the bill of sale. The manager produced the flight manual, logbook, and service manual along with the bill of sale.

Al and Frieda checked all the documents and when they agreed it was what they wanted, Al wrote out a cheque for the full amount, including a fill up of fuel.

Al asked Wilbur if he would fly them in the DC3 back to the airport at Glendale. He also asked Wilbur as to how they could get it shipped to Rome or Paris.

"No problem. Douglas has special shipping containers for the DC3. I'll see that it is disassembled, stored in the container, placed aboard a freighter and shipped to whichever is the quickest and best place to ship it for reassembling. Douglas will advise on that; it might even be England as they had a lot of them over there, so that might be your best bet for shipping and getting reassembled. I'll see to it."

Before leaving on TWA at Glendale for New York, Al insisted Wilbur calculate his time and costs so he can be paid in full. Al included a bonus in his cheque for Wilbur's help and service just to make sure he had covered all his costs. They thanked him for his kindness and friendship; Al gave him his card with their Friedrichshafen address and told him to call on them if he was ever in the area.

A month later, Al received a phone call from London advising him the DC3 was assembled and ready for them at Heathrow Airport. They got a charter flight to Paris and then British Airways to London. The DC3 was sitting in front of the Heathrow Tower, waiting for its new owners to take it home. They filled up with petrol and filed a flight plan in the administration office. They obtained clearance from the Tower with the controller remarking, "Nice plane, have a safe trip home. Captains Wirth cleared for take-off. Come again."

"Thank you, Heathrow Tower--appreciate the hospitality."

"I guess several of them got a peek at this luxury plane and someone might have even remembered us from the days we used to fly in here with Lufthansa. I know for sure they remember the famous Frieda and also they saw your name on the flight plan. It pays to be married to a famous aviatrix who is flying our plane home."

They landed at Paris, topped up the tanks with petrol, advised the Tower of their destination and ETA (Estimated Time of Arrival), received clearance and took off for the Friedrichshafen Airport. They had phoned Albert from Paris and asked him to bring the auto to the airport and pick them up.

He was at the door of the plane with the wheel steps to greet them and as soon as they opened the door he leaped inside the plane. He wanted to see the new family toy and he was very pleased at what he saw. Frieda had to grab him to get her welcome home kiss; he was all eyes for the plane. All the way home all he could talk about was the plane and where they were going to fly it. That's when Frieda and Al realized there was soon going to another pilot in the house.

At dinner time, Frieda and Al decided the plane should have a name. They were discussing it when Albert said, "What was the name of the plane you escaped in from Germany?"

Al and Frieda looked at each other with blank looks; they had never discussed their escape in front of Albert.

"It was named Condor by the manufacturer. Where did you hear about our escape?"

"From Jose's and Eva's children. They knew all about how you two escaped and told me about it, and I heard Uncle Peter and Uncle Em talking about it, how you saved Lufthansa by getting the plane out of Germany before it could be destroyed. I suggest you two call it Condor ll and get a plaque engraved with that name and place it on the bulkhead in the plane."

Frieda and Al give each other a relieved look. For several years they had been discussing how to tell Albert about their escape.

Al said, "What do you think Frieda? Do you think Albert's suggestion is appropriate?"

"Yes, thank you Albert. That solves the situation."

They clinked their wine glasses and with smiles cheered, "Here's to Condor II."

In 1963 they joined the private Flying Club in Friedrichshafen; it was quite different from the Berlin Flying Club of 1935. A lot of the members had their own planes: everything from twin engine executive planes to the single engine light planes used for rental use to Club members and for instructing new students.

Albert was signed on for instruction in the summer of 1964 while he was on his summer break from the university in Munich, where he was studying medicine. By the end of the summer he had got enough flying time and passed all the necessary courses to obtain his commercial ticket. Now, after being properly checked out, he could co-pilot on the DC3 for either his mother or his father pilots.

In November of 1964 they got a phone call from Wilbur Wright who was in Paris on a holiday. Al asked him if he could stay a few days with them, and if so he and Albert would fly over to Paris and pick him up. Wilbur said he would enjoy that. Al and Albert flew over to Paris that afternoon and picked up Wilbur. Albert had never been to the Paris Airport where there was heavy air traffic and a no nonsense Control Tower. It was good experience for him.

After Al introduced Albert to Wilbur, Al asked Wilbur if he would take the captain's seat to fly the plane back to Friedrichshafen. He wanted Albert to be co-pilot to this master pilot of DC3s.

The way Wilbur talked to the Paris Tower made Al ask if he had flown from there before.

Wilbur said, "Oh, I haven't told you yet. I'm a captain on Pan Am now, flying DC8s. I've flown to Paris several times, also Rome and London. I'm just taking a holiday, using my flight pass."

During the flight he gave Albert several pieces of information about the DC3.

He said with a wink and a smile, "I didn't tell your mother or father everything about this baby when we were testing it because they might not have bought it. I can tell about a couple of its quirks, just in case you ever run into them."

Albert was very impressed with Wilbur and hung on to every word about the plane and listened to Wilbur talk about flying into all the different places around the world.

On the flight he handed Al an airplane magazine which had write-ups about some new executive type jets that have just come on the market. One of the pages had a corner folded; it was a write-up about a plane called a Lear Jet. The specs on this plane intrigued Al and he asked Wilbur if he had seen one. Wilbur said he had not only seen one but he had flown two of them from the factory to customers.

"What do you think about this jet plane?"

"Al, I have flown a lot of different planes, but this jet is by far the best. A lot of corporations are ordering them because they have a long range and save a lot of time because they are so fast. Now might be the time to trade this baby in while there is a market for it. I'm sure there is an agent in Paris--it might be worth looking into."

Frieda was glad to see Wilbur as he was part of the airplane fraternity she and Al belonged to, and they all talked the same language and enjoyed one another's company.

Frieda had to ask, "Are you married, Wilbur?"

"Not now. I was during the War, but I got lucky, she ran off with a sailor when I was busy flying the Hump. No, I was a wandering flyer. No time to settle down. Besides my real love is airplanes but I have a nice companion, Lily, in Los Angeles. She understands me and lets me be an airplane bum. We'll probably settle down together when I retire from Pan Am."

Al and Albert flew Wilbur back to Paris with Wilbur piloting the DC3 and Albert being co-pilot. The main topic during the flight was about Wilbur's experience flying the Lear Jet and the statistics of that wonderful plane. When getting ready to fly back home, Al told Albert to fly the DC3 with Al being co-pilot and giving Albert instruction on how to depart from a large International Airport.

Just after they arrived home Frieda took a phone call from Marie. She was sobbing and gave Frieda the bad news. Em had just passed away; he had a heart attack and died suddenly. Frieda consoled her and told her they would be there tomorrow to give her a hand.

Early the next day they took off for Rinsque. On the flight down they talked of many things and Frieda asked Al about what would happen to REAAFCO.

Chapter 14

"WELL IT IS fairly simple. I'll have to buy out Em's share. Marie will be well off; she was already rich before she married Em and so money is no problem. I'm going to ask her if she will accept a cash settlement or let us string out the payments for her share, rather than take the full amount and strap the company for cash. We had the same problem when Karl wanted to cash in his shares in the company. The problem is we have most of our money tied up in investments and property; we would have to take a considerable loss to get liquid cash to pay her off. When we explained it to Karl he gladly accepted the cash settlement. We should take her back home with us when things are all settled in Rinsque. She'd probably want to settle down in Paris anyway--she has lots of friends there. Also the company lawyer who will handle everything for her is in Switzerland. I'll get him to come to our place as it'll be a lot more convenient for her, and also everything can be done from our home while she is staying there."

Both Al and Frieda felt very bad at the loss of Em. He was a true friend. It was he who made everything they possible. It was

Em who master-minded the whole plan and was the host of their wedding.

Albert flew the plane with Al being co-pilot. Al kept thinking about that Lear Jet. If they had it now on this trip it would only take a few hours instead of taking all day in the Condor Two. Al made up his mind when Albert mentioned to him, that they should get the Lear Jet; they could save time and go further in the Lear.

After they got things settled and said their goodbyes to Em they brought Marie back home with them. This was the second husband Marie has lost; her first was in a mining accident in Africa. Neither one was easy for her. The Wirths kept her busy shopping and travelling to Paris to visit friends and relatives, and finally she told Al to get the lawyer. It was time to settle the business affairs.

Later, the lawyer told Al that she didn't really want to take any amount out of the firm, knowing it would come out of Al's pocket. She stated these were good friends and she didn't want to jeopardize the friendship. The lawyer persuaded her to accept a reasonable offer, which would be in good faith with everyone.

Frieda and Al helped her get settled in Paris near her friends with instructions to phone often and let them know when she wants to visit them. They would pick her up.

It was in April of 1965 that Al phoned the factory number for the Lear Company. A man answered: "Bill here."

"Is this the Lear Jet Company?"

"Yep, I'm Bill Lear. What can I do for you?'

"I was talking to a friend, Wilbur Wright, about your jet. I'm interested in buying one. Will you send me information and specs along with prices and availability?"

Al gave him his address hoping to hear from him soon.

Wilbur phoned later on that day and said, "I told Bill Lear what you should have in the plane, what it will be used for and for him to include two wing tanks with it so I can deliver it to Friedrichshafen. He is going to phone you and give you the details. I persuaded him to put it in ahead of some other orders, otherwise you'll go for a Capproni instead. He'll give you all the details, probably tomorrow, and I'm looking forward to delivering one and checking all of you out in it. I told Bill Lear who you two were and he realized it'll be a big feather in his cap to have you two who are well known in Europe aviation circles to own a Lear Jet. He's been trying to break into that market for some time. He's going to make sure you get his best model with all the whistles and bells! It's a beautiful plane you all will love it."

The next day Bill Lear phoned Al and gave him the details.

Al told him to proceed with the order as soon as the bank draft for the deposit was deposited in Lear's bank.

On June 15, 1965 Wilbur phoned Al to tell him he was leaving Reno, Nevada, with his plane, he was going to lay over in London and will be in Friedrichshafen in time for lunch tomorrow. Their new plane landed at 11:45 AM. They all had lunch in the Clubhouse with all the Club members looking out at the new jet and wishing they had one.

That afternoon Wilbur gave each of them instruction on this marvelous plane. Even though it was very fast it could land at most airports without any trouble, and with the wing tanks it had a very long range. The electronics in it were state of the art for navigation and communication.

After three days of instruction for all three pilots, Wilbur was flown to Paris in the Lear where he boarded a Pan Am flight using his company pass.

One night at supper Al asked Albert if he was really set on being a doctor.

Albert asked Al what he had in mind about his education.

Al said, "I think Frieda can answer the question about being a doctor better than anyone. After all she was a nurse at one time."

Frieda and Al had had some serious discussions about Albert's future and they both agreed it really wasn't the best thing for Albert to become a doctor. There were several things he could accomplish for a successful life. There are many opportunities open to him.

Frieda asked Albert, "Do you like flying planes?"

"Yes."

"Do you like skiing in the Alps?"

"Yes."

"If you are to become a doctor you'll have to give all that up."

"You know, some day you will have to take over our business interests and being a doctor you will not have time to handle that—think about it."

Frieda and Al were concerned about Albert using his time at the university studying medicine, even though they realized he would make a good doctor and it would be nice for their egos to say their son is a doctor. They were looking ahead as to what his future will be and what is best for him.

They both realized they weren't convincing him, so they dropped the subject. Maybe they were mistaken and Albert had got his heart set on being a doctor. As far as the running of the company, Al had offers on REAAFCO and he was seriously thinking of selling it off and just being an investor. It was less worry and their investment brokers would have to do the work of investing. They decided to back off because after all Albert was now an adult; the world was his plum, let him enjoy doing what he wants to do. Maybe fate might decide his future.

That winter Albert went skiing in the Austrian Alps at Innsbruck. He was taking a week's holiday and staying at a chalet up on the mountain. There were several young people enjoying the skiing and the social life.

Chapter 15

ONE NIGHT A girl he knew who was in his class at the university was there with her boy friend and she introduced him to a girl friend of hers whose name was Catherine Diener. She was blond and very pretty. She realized Albert was too shy to meet the girls. She had been watching him for two nights and finally asked her girlfriend to introduce them when she realized her friend knew him and Albert was not with a girl. It followed the same scenario as his parents: Frieda Schmidt made the move to meet the handsome pilot at that party at Dusseldorf in 1935.

Right away Catherine and Albert took a liking to each other without her knowing that his family was quite wealthy. They talked a lot about what they were taking at the university in Munich. Her discipline was in business economics and she was quite enthusiastic about it. When she found out that Albert was going in for medicine she said: "That is a noble discipline, but I think there is a better future in the business world of economics. My father is a baker in Munich and he claims if you want to get ahead in this world you have to get to know and understand business. What does your father do?"

"Oh, he is just a retired pilot."

"Was it their idea for you to go into medicine?"

"Well, not really, although mother used to be a nurse before she became a flight attendant. I guess I kind of got it from her-- maybe I'm inclined that way. So you think business economics is a better course to get ahead in this world than medicine?"

"Yes I do. Why don't you sit in on a few lectures to see for yourself. How far are you into the med course?"

"Just the first year of pre med. Will your Professor allow an outsider student sitting in on his lectures?"

"Sure, he welcomes it because it means his lectures are interesting and he is attracting new students to his discipline. I'm staying here over the weekend. How about you? I'd like to hear more about you."

"Yes, I'm here for the weekend also. Can I take you to dinner tonight?"

"OK, I was going to go with that other group, but I'd rather be with you. I promise I won't order anything expensive."

"You can order anything you want. I got a good bonus this week and I want to spend it celebrating."

"What are you celebrating? What kind of work do you do?"

"The celebration is meeting you."

"OK, but what kind of work do you do?"

"I've got a pilot's license and I do the odd job acting as co-pilot on some charter flights. Do you live in Munich? I'd like to know more about you. Have you got a boy friend?"

They had dinner that night in the chalet dining room and he insisted she order the most expensive item on the menu. She noticed he signed for everything instead of paying cash. He lied when she questioned him about it and said his father had an account at the chalet so he just put everything on it and settles up later with his father. After dinner they went into the tavern section where there was dancing. Albert had never learned to dance, so

Catherine taught him how to dance and he loved it. They had a wonderful night dancing and enjoying each other's company.

The next day was Sunday. They had agreed to meet in the dining room for breakfast at 9:30 AM. They were late getting to bed the night before and both had a good night's sleep.

They ate a hearty breakfast of fruit juice, ham and eggs, toast with jam and coffee. Albert insisted all the treats will be on him today to celebrate his meeting Catherine.

They were both good skiers and enjoyed the slopes. They stopped for a beer and sandwich at 1:30, and were on the slopes again until 4:00, then they went into the chalet and sat next to the big centre fire pit, getting warmed up and enjoying each other's company.

"Have you got a boy friend?"

"Not now. I started to go with a fellow at the university, but I broke it off."

"Why?"

"He got mean and overbearing. I became afraid of him after he hit me and also he wanted me to quit university because he wasn't going to make it to graduation."

"Sounds like a bully. Is he still going to school?"

"No, thank goodness and I haven't seen him around for some time. How about you? Where do you live and do you have a girl friend?"

"Well, let's see. I was born in Argentina, lived there until I was twelve, I speak four languages, moved to Friedrichshafen from Argentina, got my pilot's license two years ago and, yes, I have a girlfriend."

Catherine's heart sank and her face took on a hurt look.

"Who is she?"

"She goes to the Munich University. Her father is a baker and she is very pretty."

Even though there were several people in the room Catherine leaned over and threw her arms around him and gave him a big loving kiss. The girl friend that introduced them was sitting with her boyfriend not too far away. When she witnessed the kiss she clapped her hands and so did some of the other friends who knew Catherine. They were glad to see her get a boyfriend that she deserved, one who would treat her right. They had all been watching these two since they were introduced. Several of the other girls kind of wished they could have snagged this tall good-looking guy that was obviously a good catch by the way he was treating Catherine. Nobody knew much about him; none of them were aware that he was quite rich. He would rather that it would be kept his secret. He realized he was going to have to lie to Catherine about his wealth until the proper time came to reveal it. He got her phone number and promised to phone her soon. She suggested he call her Cathy, like all her friends do.

Just after he returned home, Frieda said to Al, "I think Albert has met a girl."

"Why do you say that?"

"I can tell. He is acting a little different."

At supper that night Frieda asked Albert, "Did you meet somebody on your skiing holiday?"

"Yes, I met a very nice girl. Her name is Cathy Diener. She's going to the university in Munich and she lives in Munich."

"Is she going in for medicine?"

"No, she is taking the business course."

Al asked, "What does her father do?"

All Cathy had said was that her father was a baker. He didn't know if he owned a bakeshop or was the baker in another shop. Albert didn't care--he was in love.

"I'm not sure. I think he owns a bake shop because he has talked Cathy into taking the business course."

Frieda and Al smiled at each other, satisfied with the news about Albert's selection for a girl friend. They were not the least bit snobbish about who they fraternized with, as a matter of fact they had learned through experience to avoid the social climbers. Their best friends had always been regular every day people.

Frieda said, "You'll have to bring her here for supper so we can meet her. She sounds like a nice girl. We are pleased that you met a nice girl."

The next weekend Albert phoned Cathy and got her address, then he drove to Munich to pick her up to go skiing. The father was at work but he met the mother and she invited him to have supper with them on Sunday evening after he and Cathy got back from skiing. He was going to have to pass their test on Sunday, probably have to do some more lying about his family's interests and also meet Cathy's younger brother.

Cathy and Albert had a very enjoyable time skiing and enjoying the social life of the young people. There was no mention of sleeping together even though several of the others were doing it. The only incident was when her old boy friend showed up and got verbally abusive with Cathy while she and Albert were sitting on the bench around the center fire pit. Albert told him to buzz off and not come near Cathy. The idiot went to take a poke at Albert but he telegraphed his swing to hit Albert while Albert was sitting down. Albert gave him a quick punch in the belly with his left fist, then a quick sock to the jaw with his right. The culprit crashed backwards into some chairs, breaking them. Albert grabbed the guy by the neck and the seat of his pants and threw him out the door with a warning to never go near Cathy again. When the owner of the tavern came over to them, Albert told the owner to put the damage on his bill. But the owner, instead, shook his hand and thanked him. Evidently that old boy friend has been causing trouble here before. The owner said, "You did us a great favour – forget it. Your next round is on me."

Albert met the family that night at supper. The father was a nice, friendly person and they both took a liking to each other. He was a good-natured jovial person. He asked Albert about his discipline at the university and asked, "Are you going to be a doctor?"

"Well, now I'm not sure. I think Cathy has talked me out of it. She wants me to take the same course she is taking."

Cathy changed the subject by stating that Albert was an airplane pilot. That sparked the young brother into action as he was an airplane buff. He quizzed Albert all about the airplanes he had flown, and then he asked, "What is your last name?"

Albert sensed what was coming but it was too late.

Erich asked, "Is your mother the famous German aviatrix?"

Albert, smiling, said, "Yes, Erich, that's my mother and my father is also a pilot. I guess it runs in the family." Albert had to change the subject, Erich was getting too close to what Albert didn't want to divulge.

"What are you taking up at school, Erich?"

"I'm specializing in electricity in High School."

"Are you going to take electrical engineering at the University?"

"Yes, I hope so--depends on my marks."

"Erich, there is going to be a great demand for electrical engineers. Oil and electricity are the energy sources for the world. You could do very well by being an electrical engineer. Keep at it, it's a great profession."

Albert noticed the mother and father smiling. The father said, "Thank you Albert."

When he was ready to go home, Cathy walked Albert to his car, got in to give him his good night kiss and said, "That was very nice what you said to Erich. I realize you were changing the subject when Erich started to talk about your famous family. I have a feeling there is more to you than you are letting on--however it was very nice of you and I'm sure mother and father approve of you. So do I, it has been a great day, thank you. When do I get to meet your folks?"

He said it would be soon and gave her a goodnight kiss.

During the week he phoned her and suggested he take her to her house after their classes on Friday so she could pick up her clothes and ski equipment. He wanted to take her home to his place for supper on Friday night to meet his parents, stay the night, and then they could go skiing Saturday and Sunday.

Cathy was nervous and full of questions about what to wear, what kind of house he lived in and what if his parents didn't approve of her.

Albert laughed and said, "They are no different to your parents. I guarantee you will all take a liking to each other – trust me."

When they turned up the driveway to the mansion, Cathy let out a gasp. She said, "Is this your place?"

"Yes, they got it at a bargain price when real estate was going cheap. They used the money from the sale of their house in Argentina to bid on it. Here, hold my hand, I don't want you bolting away on me."

They went into the den where Al was sitting opposite a cozy fire in the fire place, reading the paper. As he rose to meet Cathy, Frieda came in. Albert noticed she was wearing an apron even though they had a cook; it was something he had never seen her do before. He realized his mother was trying to put Cathy at ease. Both the parents give Cathy a warm welcome and made her feel comfortable right away. Albert didn't know it but Frieda and Al both visited Mr. Diener's bake shop, bought some of his products and even had a brief discussion with him about business in Munich and conditions. They both liked him and now they were meeting the daughter. So far she was not only beautiful but also intelligent and nice. They had a relaxing supper served by Frieda. The main topic was education and Cathy's future plans which she enjoyed discussing. They were quite pleased with her and later on when alone, even discussed between themselves the possibility of a marriage and that Cathy could eventually be an asset to their business.

Before going skiing on Saturday Cathy bugged Albert into letting her see the plane he flies. So instead of going direct to the ski slopes he took her to see the Lear Jet stored at the airport. When they were sitting in the cabin section of the jet she noticed a plaque on the bulkhead with the words "CONDOR THREE."

"Is that the name of this Jet?"

"Well, the make of the plane is Lear, but the owner has named his planes after a famous German plane, The Focke Wulf Condor. I can't take you up in this one now. Maybe at another time, but I can take you up in one of the Club planes."

He signed out a Cessna light plane from the Club, gassed it up, gave it a pre-flight inspection, then got her in and buckled up. He flew up over the mountains giving her the first flight she had had in an airplane with a spectacular view of the Alps and the ski slope where they would be skiing that afternoon. Luckily it was a clear day, so she had a good sightseeing trip for her first flight.

On the drive from the Airport to the ski chalet she said, "You know, you continue to amaze me. You have never had a girl friend before, you speak several languages, you're a pilot and appear to be well off. It all seems too good to be true. Am I ever glad we were introduced.

Is your father retired? Does he still fly, or is he involved in a business? I know I am getting nosy, but there seems to be a lot I don't know about you, for instance, the way you socked that bully at the chalet."

"Well, ever since we got back from Argentina I've been too busy at the university with studies; you were the first girl I was introduced to. As for my father, yes, he still flies once in a while. He has been successful investing in the stock market and that seems to be his main interest. Like your father he is pleased that I am thinking about taking the business course. As for boxing, I took that at high school. Came in handy, didn't it?"

Albert went to two of Cathy's classes and got the business bug. The professor was very good at his trade, and he made the classes very interesting. It felt the same as how his mother felt when she gave up nursing to learn how to fly an airplane; it was a lot more interesting and certainly easier. Cathy coached him on the sessions he missed before starting the course. They stayed late, studying in the library presenting scenarios to each other and legal technicalities. They became the top team in the class, each writing their own papers and getting top marks.

It was in the winter of 1968 while on an Easter break from the university, that Albert presented a big diamond ring to Cathy while they were sitting in the tavern section of the chalet. He asked, "Will you please marry me?"

Several of their gang were watching and could hear them. When she said yes, a big cheer went up and Albert gave the bar tender a nod. Champagne was served to everybody in the tavern and there was a happy celebration.

One of her girl friends said to her, "Is tonight the night?"

"Yes it is, and I am going to make sure it is. I've come prepared for this night for two years. I've held him off too long, he gets it tonight."

"You're lucky you didn't lose him. I know several of the sex machines that had their eyes on him and would have given their eye teeth to hop into bed with him."

"Well, tonight I'm making sure those temptations are eliminated, I hope."

On June 15, 1969, just after their graduation, they were married in the garden of the Wirth mansion and the reception was held in the mansion. Frieda had Cathy's father make a special big wedding cake and provide all the fancy pastries. There were several dignitary friends of the family as well as their classmate friends, and, of course, the ski gang attending the wedding. It was the best party ever held in the mansion. Cathy's father received several orders for special wedding cakes and other orders from this wedding; it set him up in a more prosperous business.

Albert flew the Condor III to Majorca for their honeymoon. They had a wonderful time swimming in the ocean. making love in the honeymoon suite each night and just relaxing on the beach discussing what their future would be in the business world.

Albert said, "Let's use your father's business as an example of what can be done to expand an ordinary small operation into a highly successful business. After all we are top graduates of the business course."

For the rest of the week they spent a lot of their spare time working out scenarios of how to expand the Diener Bake Shop business. They made a list of steps to be taken and market potential.

What is the market size? i.e., Greater Munich population?

What products required selling to the potential market?

What equipment and facility is required?

Start with a small basic operation of mass-producing.

Obtain financing to set up basic plant with provisions to expand.

Parlay excess funds into larger plant.

With extra income build plants in other nearby cities.

When ready to retire, sell off to large corporation.

Place excess funds in investment, such as real estate property, etc.

Retire rich.

When they got back they stayed at the mansion until Al bought them a nice home in the residential area of Munich. Several times in the following months they had Cathy's parents over for dinner and each time they discussed the expansion of the bakery business. They laid out a complete study and plan to go step by step for Mr. Diener to follow. They suggested starting with the original bakeshop. Cathy and Albert canvassed the wholesalers of bakery supplies in Munich. They got the lowest prices for large volume wholesale purchases of their products after Mr. Diener installed some machinery to increase production. Albert and Cathy obtained prices and specifications on the availability of the latest and best bakery equipment from their suppliers. Then they took Mr. Diener to the local bank where they arranged for financing, with Albert signing as guarantor.

Within a year Mr. Diener had to move to a larger facility. His path to success and wealth was set, thanks to his daughter's business course.

One evening after dinner, Cathy said, "We know all about my folks' business, but I haven't got a clue about your family's business. Can we talk about it, or would you rather not? I think that possibly I should know for posterity's sake?"

"You are right, Cathy. You should know and with your knowledge and ambition you could be an asset to the Wirth business."

"It started many years ago when dad was the president of Lufthansa, he and a sheik in a place called Rinsque in French West Africa where we set up a fueling business for the airlines that were flying the South Atlantic and along the African Coast. It prospered even through the war. Uncle Em, the Sheik, died a few years ago and dad bought out his share and operated the business himself until he sold out two years ago to a large corporation. He placed the funds in the hands of investment companies which pay a comfortable interest return."

"You know Albert, we got my father going on the road to wealth. I can see a huge potential with the Wirth fortune. Let's be investment advisors again and analyze your folks' business. Maybe we can do something for it, or maybe 'if it's not broke, don't fix it' approach, let it just pile up the wealth. Might be worth looking at."

They had a meeting with Al and Frieda one evening after supper. Al purposely only revealed half of the value of their investment, but it was enough to make the two business experts think and discuss the different aspects of the business. One of the things Cathy mentioned was that the business was trapped in the Swiss bank accounts under private names and numbers. If they were to form a corporation they could buy other interests outside of Switzerland under a corporation name and not be liable for individual loss or debt. It would also lower the tax rate.

Al suggested both Albert and Cathy draw up a proposal so he and Frieda could study it and think it over.

After a week of going over all the aspects of forming a corporation, they made up a complete summary of the benefits and how to go about forming the corporation.

They had Frieda and Al over for dinner one night and presented their proposal after dinner. Both Al and Frieda read the proposal carefully and they both agreed that they should go ahead with the plan.

Al asked, "Any idea what the corporation should be called?"

Cathy said, "I understand the plan you had to get out of Germany was referred to as 'OPERATION CONDOR'. How about 'OPCON CORPORATION'?"

Frieda and Al let out a big laugh and each hugged Cathy as the final welcome into the Wirth Empire. She chose that time to announce that she was expecting their grandchild.

THE FOCKE WULF FW 200 CONDOR

The Condor was designed for the Deutsche Lufthansa which wanted an airliner for a route to South America. Its high aspect ratio and long span wing was characteristic of long range aircraft, sail planes, and the Condor bird that the aircraft was named after. Its modern flush-riveted, light alloy construction aimed for maximum efficiency. It was intended to fly 26 passengers over long distances as was demonstrated in August 1938 by a flight from Berlin to New York City in 20 hours non-stop.

Production began in 1938 with the FW 200A-O transports. One of them became Hitler's personal aircraft, registered as D-2600 and named the "Immelmann II" after the German ace from World War I.